I0537379

THE
SAGITTARIUS
MYSTERIES

Inner Vision

Adrian Holland

Published by AMAZOLA

The right of Adrian Holland to be identified as the Author of the work has been asserted by him in accordance with the Copyright, Design and Patents Act 1988.

Copyright © Adrian Holland 2013

ISBN 978-1-909466-19-7

All rights reserved. No part of this publication may be reproduced, stored in a retrieval system, or transmitted in any form or by means, electronic, mechanical, photocopying, recording, or otherwise, without the prior permission of the publishers.

For further information please contact the official website at

www.amazolapublishing.com

A copy of this book is held at the British Library.

Cover design illustrations by Adrian Holland

I was very close to both of my parents who were my best friends, and I have lost count of the number of happy times we shared, and all of the creativity and laughter. Like my beloved father Joe, my mother Margaret was so special, and my total inspiration. I would therefore like to dedicate this book to their memory.

Contents

Introduction

"*Brandon Sagittarius*, is he American?"

"No British."

"Unusual name!"

"Unusual sort of a chap. His grandfather was a *boffin* at Bletchley Park, solving the *Enigma Code* - seems as though he is a bit of an *enigma* himself!"

"What do you mean?"

"Well, he's head of *Experimental*."

"Experimental?"

"Yes, that's the department responsible for all of the gadgets used by MI6."

"Bit of a spy then."

"No, not really."

"Just in charge of exploding pens and poisoned tipped umbrellas, that sort of thing."

"Even so, it all sounds a bit odd."

"Yes, very!"

"So, is he our man?"

"Well, it does seem like our best option, so let's give him a call."

One

"Hello professor?"

"Yes."

"We seem to have a bit of a problem, and I wondered if you could help..."

The professor took a deep breath adjusting his tinted glasses with his left hand, as his right held onto the receiver. He listened intently, as the well-spoken voice hesitantly conversed with him from the other end of the telephone.

Sagittarius had a reputation for being intense, with an unfathomable aura around him. *Enigma* was indeed an apt description of him, and he had a way of making anyone who dealt with him feel ill at ease. He had the ability to literally *see through* people and they knew it, but his unique talents were the things that forced them into his proverbial *Lions Den.*

Most people settled for the relative safety of the telephone, though this gave them little comfort as they could still feel his presence probing their innermost secrets. He was even more foreboding in person, as his intensity instantly placed the most robust individual onto the defensive.

Standing just over six feet in height, his large build seemed to project power, along with his tailored image. He always wore a black pinstriped Savile Row suit, white shirt, red paisley cravat, and black Chelsea boots. The boots gave him an extra inch, and they were always shiny and just as sharp as his suit. His dark shoulder-length black wavy hair was always immaculately swept back, which contrasted with his usual light stubble. However, it was his designer tinted glasses that hid his dark brown eyes which always gave him the appearance of an assassin. This was not helped by a natural light tan, and although he was English, it gave him a continental appearance.

He listened to what was being said, letting his mind wander along the telephone line to the receiver on the other end. He sensed hesitancy, along with several guarded secrets. He also sensed distrust, and the fact that information was being withheld from him. In his mind he could see a greying man of small stature sitting in a *chesterfield* at a *Gentleman's Club*, discussing matters with an older balding man. They were definitely colluding in something, and whatever it was, there was more than a little deception going on!

Sagittarius listened without comment as the voice at the other end of the telephone reached the conclusion of the one-sided conversation, and when it was over, there was a long pause. He could sense that the interlude was unsettling the caller, which was his intention!

It was also clear that it was non-negotiable, as it came from the upper reaches of *Whitehall*.

"I see."

Sagittarius replied, before putting the telephone receiver down.

There was a lot of squirming at the other end, followed by a loud out flowing of breath.

"Did he take the bait?"

"I think so."

"Let's just hope he doesn't bring that damned rabbit with him!"

Two

"Well, what do you think Oracle?"

There was a twitching of whiskers, on the nose of a large black rabbit which sat on the desk next to Sagittarius, indicating that they were both in agreement.

"An inoculation!"

There was another twitch of whiskers. The thought of it brought back unhappy memories of his short time at school - very short as it had turned out. At the school medical they had forced him to have the *measles vaccine*, which caused a bad reaction, and he refused to go back. His legendary stubbornness caused his parents all sorts of problems, resulting in him being educated at home.

His upbringing was far from what you might term *conventional*, and had resulted in him being a bit of a *loner*. That was the way he liked it, and being forced to have an inoculation resonated uncomfortably with him, and his *gut feeling* placed him on his guard.

Oracle also had the same feeling, opening his eyes a little wider.

Sagittarius reached down for his black *Gladstone bag*, placing it on the desk. Oracle looked at him, realising that he was going undercover, and felt a pair of large powerful hands gently lifting him into its carefully prepared interior. Closing it gently, he reached for his raincoat which hung on the coat stand next to his umbrella. It was also black, and he slipped it on, grabbing the umbrella before reaching for the bag.

"Keep your sense sharp; we need to gather more information."

Oracle looked at him through the special material, which enabled him to see out, but no one to see in, as they headed for the door. The corridor was quite bright, in contrast to the sombre oak door which held a brass nameplate.

EXPERIMENTAL DEPT HEAD

PROFESSOR B. SAGITTARIUS

The lift pinged, the door slid open, and they entered. There were two people inside involved in a conversation which suddenly died when they saw him. Sagittarius barely acknowledged them as worried looks appeared on their faces. They could see the bag and knew that it was more than their lives were worth to comment, or even to raise an eyebrow. Sagittarius was not one to cross!

It was unusual to say the least, having a large black rabbit for a companion, particularly carrying it about in a black *Gladstone bag*. But Oracle was no ordinary rabbit; in fact he was an extraordinary creation. Oracle was a *Cyber Rabbit*, who had taken more that thirty years of evolution. No one knew of his exact identity, naturally assuming that he was real and not artificial. Everyone assumed that Sagittarius was eccentric, just like his *boffin* grandfather, and would have been shocked if they had known the real truth.

Oracle possessed a lot of highly specified secret technology which was beyond most people's comprehension. Even some of the greatest minds in this particular field would have been stumped, as it was virtually impossible to tell that he was not a real creature. The *powers that be* were also completely in the dark, but they had little choice but to accept him, as there was no one else capable of doing the job as well as Sagittarius.

The lift door pinged again, and there was a tangible sigh of relief as he left the other two occupants. When the door closed again, they resumed their conversation.

"He always puts me on edge!"

"Me too!"

"There's something very mysterious about him."

"You can say that again!"

"…and as for that rabbit!"

They kept their voices to a whisper, not realising that Oracle had picked up their conversation, transmitting it to Sagittarius, who smiled to himself. He enjoyed being a figure of mystery, but it was never of derision, as he was well respected for his intellect. He had only once been publicly ridiculed, and his lightening quick reactions had resulted in the perpetrator having a pressure point pressed and he had almost instantaneously lost conciseness and fallen to the ground. From that moment on, no one had dared to comment again!

A long corridor stretched out into the distance and led to a secret entrance, disguised in a Gentleman's Tailors. There was another door which emerged into a Ladies Hairdresser next door, both within the confines of an upmarket arcade. It was what was left from a bygone age of *espionage*, although it still had its uses. In these days of terrorism it made perfect sense not to use the front door when on a *mission*. However, Sagittarius was such a striking figure, that he was never one to simply blend into a crowd, and to most people he resembled a *Harley Street* doctor.

It was quite a long walk down the corridor, although it did give him time to stretch his legs. Sitting behind a desk was an occupational hazard for a *Head of Department*, but he relished his time in the laboratories. The last few weeks had seen an increased workload, and the endless forms and general paperwork seemed never ending. At least this would give him a break, and he hoped that it would not be long before he could resume his research.

There were several ongoing projects, all classified and very experimental. Some would eventually see the light of day, whilst others would be consigned to the storeroom. They mostly concerned software and small gadgets - very small, bordering on nano technology, as this was where the research was going these days. Many of the projects that had been undertaken over the last years had been adapted secretly to enhance Oracle's already mind boggling range of capabilities. Sagittarius smiled to himself at the thought of what the *Department* would have made of his *cyber rabbit* if ever it were to truly understand just what he was. No one had ever had the slightest idea that he was not a real creature, which was testament to his brilliance!

Fortunately, Sagittarius was not an *egotist,* otherwise he would have surely given away his secret. Oracle was his life's work, and represented a real breakthrough in technology. If his private research got into the wrong hands, then he dreaded to think of the consequences. He had built in many safeguards within his operating software, as well as many other defensive capabilities. Who would have thought that a simple black rabbit would be able to pack quite a proverbial *punch!*

Sagittarius neared the door, looking into the outdated retina scanner. There had been a lot of cutbacks and this particular model was already years out of date and overdue for replacement. Security was not as it used to be; in fact, few things were now what you might call *cutting-edge*. With a deep sigh, he placed his eye in front of the socket, waiting for it to buzz with identification, which it did after verification. The lock clicked, and he opened the steel reinforced door, before pushing his way inside.

He smiled again to himself as he entered the back room of the Gentleman's Tailors. The door closed behind him with a click, and he walked past the rows of cloth before pushing the curtain aside and emerging into the main shop, just like *Mr Ben*, one of his childhood favourites. Who would have thought that he would have been emulating the cartoon character he used to watch all of those years ago?

It was quiet today, so there was no need for subterfuge, and as he pulled the curtain back, the tailor nodded his head understandably, as he walked past acknowledging him with a nod of his own.

The main door had an antiquated bell which rang as he opened it, and the whole shop had the feel of somewhere lost in time. The bell continued to ring, as he closed the door behind him, looking over towards the mannequins displaying the fine woven cloth suits.

The arcade was quite busy, with people hustling and bustling about, totally unaware of where he had come from. Reaching down he pulled his pocket watch out of his waistcoat pocket, checking the time. It was almost exactly twelve o'clock, and time for a spot of lunch before he made the rendezvous.

Sagittarius always carried his pocket watch, although it was far from an ordinary time piece. Behind the white porcelain dial containing the black roman numerals and sculpted hands, instead of the intricate workings lay an assortment of

11

miniaturised devices. These again he had painstakingly crafted in his private laboratory at home. Sagittarius probably carried more secrets in that silver case than within the entire department, and that was the way he intended to keep it!

On the corner of the arcade was a coffee shop cum bistro, which specialised in organic food. He had often been temped, but the smell of coffee had always put him off. It was a shame, as in this day and age it was difficult to find somewhere that sold fresh food that was not processed and full of additives and chemicals, and being a vegetarian also limited where he could eat. Things had started to improve though, but he was still very choosy as to what he would eat, and where he would eat it.

The tables outside were full of people enjoying the menu on offer, and as he passed them the unmistakeable aroma of coffee greeted his upturned nostrils. He really hated the stuff, and if he had had his way, then it would have been banned. This coffee was specially ground however, and so the smell was not quite as unpleasant as it was in other establishments.

"Nice to see you again, doctor."

A pleasant waitress gave him a warm, friendly smile as she placed an order down on a nearby table.

"You're becoming a bit of a regular."

Sagittarius smiled back, although beneath the smile there was puzzlement. He had a very good memory and knew that he had not eaten there before.

"Usual is it, coffee and a bacon sandwich?"

Now this confirmed his suspicions, either she was wrong, or there was something very strange going on.

It was lunch time, and come to think about it, he did feel rather peckish. Looking at the menu board on the wall, he noticed that it did offer some tempting dishes - apart that was from coffee and a bacon sandwiches!

He thought about it for a moment, before making his decision.

"I think I will dine inside today, and by way of a change, I would like to order an apple juice and pasta with Greek salad please."

The waitress smiled at him, as he followed her into the bistro, sitting down at a table near the back. The waitress returned a few minutes later with his apple juice, smiling warmly again.

"How are you getting along at the clinic, settling into your new job I hope?"

"Very well thank you."

Sagittarius kept up the pretence, realising that she was convinced that he was somebody else.

"It is always difficult settling into a new job, and I hope that they are treating you well round the corner."

Sagittarius smiled, as she left him with a bit of a puzzle that his curiosity was determined to solve. Which particular clinic was she referring too?

He looked at Oracle, who was sitting comfortably in his Gladstone bag, on the seat next to him. They both had the same thought, which was not surprising as Sagittarius had downloaded as much information about himself as he could into his memory, helped by a neuronet which he had upgraded from one of the development programs. Strange as it might have seemed, he had been able to access virtually all of his memories which had been transferred via the skull cap's electrical impulses which had matched his own brainwave patterns. It was fair to say that Sagittarius was a genius, albeit one who had access to the latest technology in his *Experimental Department*. That came in really handy for his endeavours as there were also a lot of other brilliant minds within it too.

Information began to flash up inside his tinted glasses, firing into his brain via his optic nerve. In his mind he had a virtual image of the data being fed to him via Oracles' massive processor. The glasses had been in development for years, and were yet another piece of equipment that he had *borrowed* and improved upon.

Oracle brought up a map of the surrounding area, highlighting a private clinic just a few streets away. It was obvious that whoever the waitress thought he was must work there, and even more astonishing, that it was the very place he had been ordered to attend!

There was little information about it, only the name *INNER VISION* followed by a brief description *Private Health Clinic and Cosmetic Surgery*. There was also a contact number followed by a link to their web site. Oracle instantly brought it up, again there was little information, only the same words as on the search engine. It just showed a directory listing, contact information and a map showing its location.

Inner Vision, that was a bit of a coincidence, as that was how he was viewing the information. Sagittarius did not believe in coincidences, and his curiosity was raised to another level.

There was a clank of plates as the waitress brought his meal, and the display on the inside of his glasses began to fade. She was smiling again, obviously showing quite an interest in him. She was in her early twenties, slim and attractive with shoulder length blonde hair tied back in a pony tail. He could also sense that behind the outer layer of self confidence, there was vulnerability, and a personality conflict going on. He also sensed that in some way she was attracted to him, even though he was old enough to be her father!

Sagittarius was a bachelor, with no time for relationships, only work. Oracle had taken up most of his spare time outside of his working hours, and even though he was virtually complete, there were always ways of enhancing his already considerable abilities.

He was briefly distracted by the television which hung from a bracket on the far wall. It had been tuned into one of the 24 hour news channels, and there was a report of a possible pandemic.

Scientist predict that it is only a matter of time before there is an outbreak of the so called 'Bat Flu'. It is alleged that there has already been one case reported which is being treated in a private health clinic here in London.

The waitress sighed.

"First we had *Chicken Flu*, then *Pig Flu*, and now we have *Bat Flu*."

Sagittarius nodded.

"...and they say that it could just be around the corner, literally!"

He froze, there was another coincidence, right place, right time!

"I'm sure that there is no cause for alarm."

He tried to sound reassuring, although alarm bells were ringing inside his head.

There was just something unusual about her, as if part of her was trying to tell him something - warn him, and yet trap him both at the same time. He always prided himself on being a good judge of character, and studied her more closely as he continued with their conversation.

"I would not be too worried."

Looking at her name badge he added.

"Gemini."

She blushed.

"My parents led an alternative lifestyle.

He smiled, and breaking his golden rule, he gave a little information about himself.

"I know the feeling!"

He stood up, offering her his hand.

"Brandon, Brandon Sagittarius."

Gemini began to laugh.

"I'm so glad that I'm not on my own!"

This was the first time that he felt as though he had found a kindred spirit, and he remembered overhearing the conversation at his interview, when he had been recruited.

Oracle was still under development in those days, and his processor had been discretely placed in his suit's inner pocket.

Little did his interviewers realise that he had been *eaves dropping* on their conversation from the corridor outside.

"…and who do we have next?

"A chap named Sagittarius."

"Sagittarius?"

"Yes."

"How odd!"

"Parents were those hippie types."

"How awful!"

"Father changed his surname in the sixties…"

"Are you sure we want that type here?"

"Apparently he's an absolute genius."

"Genius or not, are you sure?"

"Well, there's only one way to find out!"

"You had better bring him in then!"

From that moment an uncomfortable relationship had developed between the *old school tie brigade* and Sagittarius, whose education had been somewhat different!

They treated him as a bit of a *maverick*, realising that they had little choice but to employ him, as there was no one else who possessed his intellect or abilities. Sagittarius would never have entertained the idea of working for them, if it had not been the fact that he now had access to the level of technology required to complete Oracle.

"You seem a little different today!"

Gemini looked confused, as the battle within her raged on.

"Well, we all have our *doppelgängers*!"

She laughed, although underneath she looked worried by his remark.

"I'm so glad that you didn't order a coffee today. I shouldn't say it, but the smell turns my stomach, but I need the job so I have to put up with it!"

It seemed as though, having been initially way off the mark, she was now homing in on his likes and dislikes.

"You wouldn't be a vegetarian by any chance would you?"

"Yes, how can you tell?"

"Lucky guess!"

She blushed as if she was trying to hide something, feeling his presence within her troubled mind. It went further than perception, a calming influence, stilling the choppy waters within an ocean of confusion.

"So tell me about my other self?"

Gemini felt as though she was being manipulated, and there was nothing that she could do to resist, as they continued with their conversation.

"It must be over a month since you first came in, and you were a lot different to the way you are now. Your clothes for a start. You wore a dull grey suit, with a dull grey tie."

She felt as though he could sense that she was lying, and cringed inwardly. Sagittarius had a dislike of grey, and never wore a tie unless he was forced too, and even then, it would never be grey!

18

Gemini had the feeling that she had made a mistake, and in an attempt to recover the situation, she began to turn the conversation around.

"Come to think about it, now that I have had a chance to have a good look at you, your features seem a little different. Maybe you do have a *doppelgänger* after all!"

They both smiled, as another customer called to her. She was glad, as she felt as though she had almost messed everything up.

"I will have to go, otherwise I will get into trouble, and I can't afford to lose this job!"

Gemini left him, and Oracle twitched his nose again, as his processor went to work, thinking the very same thoughts as Sagittarius.

The meal was delicious, and he sat in contemplation, wondering why all of these coincidences had happened. There was certainly something very strange going on, and he intended to get to the bottom of it.

She had certainly been lying, and was clearly hiding something. It felt as though she was trying to draw him in, and if he did not know any better, he would have thought that she was trying to *pick him up*.

Sagittarius checked his pocket watch; he would have to make a move if he wanted to keep the prearranged appointment. His earlier conversation was something else that he needed to think about.

Gemini took the order from a nearby table, and he indicated that he would like his bill. She smiled warmly at him, and in a few minutes she returned handing it to him.

19

Sagittarius slipped a hand into his inside pocket producing a twenty pound note.

"Keep the change."

She gratefully accepted it, thanking him for his generosity, smiling warmly at him again, and handing him his receipt.

"..And will we be seeing you again soon?"

"You never know!"

With that he picked up his Gladstone bag, umbrella and raincoat, giving her a cheery wave.

Once outside he slipped his raincoat over his shoulders, and was about to slip the receipt into his pocket, when he noticed something written on the other side.

Call me, followed by a mobile number and then *X Gemini*.

Three

Dull grey rain clouds began to fill the clear blue sky blotting out the warming rays of the sun, as a cool breeze swept along the high street. For once the weather forecast had been right in what it had said, and now looking up Sagittarius was glad that he had brought his raincoat, as it looked as though he was about to need it. What had started out as a pleasant day was rapidly going down hill, and he hoped that it was not an omen of things to come. Today had been full of coincidences, and they seemed to be piling up just like the clouds overhead. It also looked as though there was someone walking about who looked just like him - apart from liking to drink coffee and eat bacon sandwiches!

Gemini was also a little too friendly for his liking, and leaving him her number gave him a lot more to think about.

What was she really after?

Why was she interested in a man who was probably old enough to be her father?

Having said that though, Sagittarius was only in his mid forties, although he assumed that that would seem old to anyone in their early twenties. He could sense that there was a lot going on in her mind, and she was not the only one, as there was also *Inner Vision* to think about, which sounded more like an eye clinic than anything else. However, it was the telephone conversation that he had earlier with the *old school tie* that really puzzled him. Somehow, that seemed just as bizarre as the news report, which confirmed what they had talked about.

"There is a new pandemic about to break which they are calling *Bat Flu*."

Bat flu was an odd concept, particularly as most people never came into contact with bats, and even if they did, bats jaws were too weak to bite, and it was virtually unheard of for them to be able to pierce the skin. They were nocturnal creatures who lived in barns or caves, and even if they did come in contact with a human, then there was very little chance of contamination. There was a very remote chance that another animal may have eaten one, and possibly that could have entered the food chain. It was times like this, that he was glad of being a vegetarian!

"Due to the present cutbacks, we no longer have any medical facilities within the Department, and therefore we have an arrangement with a local clinic."

If funding was that tight, then why use a clinic in an exclusive part of the city, after all London prices are noted for being more expensive then anywhere else.

"Authorization has been given for all Department Heads to be inoculated as a precaution, and the *Experimental Department* is to be no exception."

The last thing that Sagittarius wished for was to have some of the *Bat Flu* virus enter his system. He was most particular of what entered his body, particularly after the nano robots.

During his research, and other research carried out within his department, nano technology had been one area which they had been focussing upon, as it offered huge possibilities. Injecting those minuscule machines into the human body offered all sorts of benefits, as they could repair all manner of things without the need for surgery. It really was a bit of a *holy grail*, and something which he knew quite a lot about. During his spare time he had spent countless hours experimenting with the whole concept, and taken research from his department to another level. Not only did it offer a way of repairing the human body, but it also offered the possibility of improving it too!

It was not so much the body that had intrigued him, but the mind. If a nano robot could be designed in such a way, then it could help to access the brain. This was something that he had been working on for several years, and, just a few short months ago he had injected himself with a syringe full of them. On reflection it did not seem the most sensible thing to do, using himself as a human *guinea pig*. He had run the risk of damaging his brain and he could have ended up as a proverbial *vegetable!*

Maybe his self confidence had crossed the border into over confidence or even arrogance, and he realised that maybe it had not been very sensible to gamble with his own life?

All thoughts of failure had soon passed as the experiment had proved to be a complete success. He now had an interface with Oracle, as the nano robots now had a direct connection with him. Every thought, be it conscious or subconscious, now entered Oracle's massive processor, and the two were inextricably linked. Who would have thought that such a thing was possible?

Cybernetics was something else that he had been working on for over thirty years, starting as a child with a simple robotic toy, and constantly enhancing it until it was able to mimic human behaviour. Sagittarius had been a loner as a child, with only his pet rabbit for company. The loss of his only real friend had devastated him, and it was from that trauma that he had focussed all of his attentions on recreating his beloved friend.

There were some who would, and indeed had questioned his sanity, but his initial grief had turned into quite an obsession.

From those early days there had been many advances in computer technology, not to mention the arrival of many new synthetic fibres. He smiled to himself as he walked along noticing a woman with very large and obviously false breasts. The very same silicon substance had been used to cover Oracle's cybernetic framework, before it had been covered with the best imitation fur that he could find. It looked and felt so real that it was almost impossible to tell the difference. The woman shivered, as she passed him, apparently the implants always remained cold even during summer, but Sagittarius had solved that problem too. Oracle's temperature was set at just the right level as any normal rabbit. He was a triumph, a technical leap forward and more importantly his trusted friend and companion!

Sagittarius turned the corner as the first spots of rain began to splatter against the pavement, a precursor for the heavy shower which was about to descend. They were enough to cause the windscreen wipers of the heavy London traffic to start to whirr back and forth like a lot of waving hands at a concert. He liked music, although that was not always the case. Being forced to learn to play the piano as a child was not much fun, but he had to admit that he was very glad of it now, as he really enjoyed playing, which was the way he liked to relax. It also gave him time to think as it freed his mind from all the calculations that usually whirred around inside his head. He liked nothing better than to sit on his piano stool with Oracle by his side losing himself in one of the classics. He frowned as music blared out of a passing car - a one bar song repeating endlessly with someone chanting something almost incomprehensible over the top.

INNER VISION, Private Health Clinic and Cosmetic Surgery

The small brass sign greeted him, as the drops of rain began to merge into the expected shower, and he hoisted his umbrella quickly. It was the only indication that the clinic existed, and if you did not look carefully then you would have missed it altogether. The outside was part of a row of Edwardian terraces, all neatly painted white, with columned entrances and balconies overlooking the busy road. Some steps led up to the large wooden door, and he could see a receptionist sitting at a desk through the glass panels. Taking a deep breath he climbed the steps pushing the front door open, and retracting the spines of his umbrella as he went. She gazed up at him with a vacant look in her eyes, as the opening door gained her attention.

There was silence as he approached her desk, and she looked as though her mind was somewhere else. He waited for her to say something, but she remained silent.

"Sagittarius."

He announced himself, and there was an uncomfortable pause as she looked up blankly from her seat, as he waited for her reply.

"We've been expecting you."

Now that her long awaited answer had arrived, his heart sank as this was the last place he wished to be. In his mind, he was already going through a variety of valid reasons why he should not have the inoculation, determined to get around the problem somehow.

The receptionist rose from her desk, a little unsteady on her feet, and he wondered whether she had been inoculated. If it did this to you, then there was absolutely no way he was going to entertain the idea. Somehow, she looked as though she was not really here, operating on *auto pilot*. She was a middle aged lady, a little plump with thick glasses which she wore on a chain. Obviously she needed them for her computer, and her tight black fitted suit bulged as she walked forward.

"I have been asked to take you in as soon as you arrive."

Reluctantly he followed her towards a door which opened to reveal a long corridor. Like all of the other properties in this row, the wealthy families had long since moved away, leaving a variety of businesses in their wake. There were still signs of the former grandeur and at least they had kept many of the original features. History and architecture were all very well, but it was why he was here that concerned him.

The receptionist led him to the rear of the building where there was a large unmarked white wooden door. She knocked on it before entering, leaving him briefly on his own, before returning.

"The doctor is ready to see you now Mr. Sagittarius."

An uneasy feeling swept over him as he sensed something was not quite right. Why would a doctor not have his name plate on his door and if they had been expecting him why had she called him Mister instead of Professor?

She opened the door for him, and he could see the doctor standing hesitantly on the other side, and as he saw Sagittarius, he approached offering his hand. His handshake was limp and his hand cold and clammy, just like a fish. He always mistrusted anyone with a weak handshake, and the man seemed to be very uncomfortable in his presence. This was not uncommon, as he had a way of unsettling people, and maybe his reputation had preceded him?

"Doctor Crawley."

"Professor Sagittarius."

Crawley or crawler?

The doctor seemed to be one of those *creepers*, the *yes men* he so despised - weak and spineless, with a thin face and equally thin body. It was fair to say that the doctor did not look at all well himself, and had a slight nervous twitch which Sagittarius found very distracting.

"Please, take a seat."

The doctor pointed to a chair, which had been placed in front of his desk. Looking round, Sagittarius could see that the room did look a little like a consulting room, although it was obviously geared up more to cosmetic surgery than for general practice. There were various certificates and a large mirror on the wall, and the desk looked quite bare, apart from a note book, and a series of leaflets advertising the clinic's services.

Behind the desk there was a cabinet with various other items in it, and on the other side of the room there was a bed, which looked as though it was used as part of the consultation process.

The doctor could see him looking around, which seemed to unsettle him even further, and when he spoke, it was with hesitancy.

"I am, uh, sure that you have heard of the new, uh, pandemic which is about to make an impact."

"Yes."

Sagittarius was his usual direct self, making the doctor twitch even more, and he looked very nervous, shuffling about, as Sagittarius sat on the chair, placing his belongings neatly on the floor besides him.

"As far as we know, it, uh, originated from Asia, and has, uh, now made its way over here. It is quite unpleasant and can cause harm to both the immune and nervous systems."

The doctor looked as though he already had it, which gave Sagittarius even less confidence in the vaccine.

"It has been agreed that all senior staff within your organisation should, uh, have the injection." He raised his eyebrows indicating that he had some knowledge of just what *organisation* Sagittarius worked for.

"I am not sure that I wish to have it!"

The doctor frowned, as Sagittarius stubbornly crossed his arms, sitting there obstinately.

"I'm afraid that, uh, it has already been decided."

Sagittarius gave him a very hard stare.

"We will see about that!"

The doctor went pale.

"Now there's no need to, uh, be like that, it's all perfectly safe. I have had the injection myself."

Sagittarius was right; the doctor looked as though he had the disease and did not look as if the injection had done him any good.

"Can we just say that I have had it, and I will live with the consequences if I do contract the disease, after all, if you already have an inoculation then surely you have a cure?"

"I'm afraid that it doesn't, uh, quite work like that!"

Sagittarius frowned, making the doctor squirm.

It was at that point that he felt as though he was being watched, and noticed what he suspected to be a two way mirror on the wall. Oracle had been feeding him information, and the consulting room was not quite what it appeared to be.

"Now then, there is no need to be difficult about it; after all I am, uh, only doing my job."

"That is as it may be, but I do not wish to have the injection."

Sagittarius had a real stubborn streak, and when his mind was made up, there was no way of changing it.

"Oh, well, uh, I'm afraid that you have little choice!"

The doctor reached into his pocket, and pressed a small emergency buzzer, and within a few moments, three rough looking men stormed into the room. Sagittarius quickly rose to his feet, as they attempted to retrain him. He was having none of it, and as three sets of arms grabbed hold of him, a scuffle developed.

Sagittarius managed to shove the first one sending him sprawling over the doctor's desk, and losing his temper he punched the second in the stomach, knocking the wind out of him. He was just about to strike the third, when he felt a sharp pain in the back of his neck, as the doctor plunged a needle into it.

This did little to calm his temper, as he lashed out again, catching the third man cleanly on the jaw, and he dropped to the floor. Then, he grabbed hold of the doctor, throwing him against the wall, before grabbing his things, and heading for the door.

Four

The red mist of temper still clouded his vision as Sagittarius strode down the corridor, his Gladstone bag and raincoat swinging from side to side. He had been determined not to have the injection, and had been tricked, despite his best efforts. He felt betrayed, angry and confused as he burst into reception, startling the receptionist who jumped aside as he rushed past her heading for the main door. Within a few moments he was standing on the pavement, his vision blurring, and his whole body trembling with rage. He was absolutely furious, although this was tempered by a realisation that his worst fears had been realised. His instinct of mistrust had been well placed, and all of those coincidences had indeed added up to the same conclusion, namely that there was something underhand going on.

He needed to get away, before they came running after him, and so he headed back towards the arcade, and the relative safety of the Tailor's shop. If he could make it there, then maybe there was someone who could help. Help was one thing, but trust was something else!

If all of this had come from higher up, then who could he trust?

If he went back to his department, then maybe they were all in on it, and *it* was something that he had not fathomed yet.

His legs seemed to have a will of their own, and driven by grim determination, he staggered on. He could feel Oracle working hard to stabilise him, although even his profound abilities seemed to be struggling. Just what had they injected him with, and more importantly why?

Somehow, he managed to make it as far as the bistro, nearly stumbling into some customers who moved aside, wondering if there was something radically wrong with him. The occupants of the nearest table also scattered as he careered towards them, like a drunk on a pub crawl. Sagittarius stumbled losing his balance, and as he fell he felt a pair of arms grabbing hold of him.

"Sagittarius, what has happened to you?"

It was the voice of the waitress Gemini, who now had her arms wrapped around him. She managed to get him to a chair, and he gratefully sat down, still holding onto his Gladstone bag and raincoat.

"Long story!"

"Do you want me to get a doctor?"

They say that a picture paints a thousand words, but the look on his face would have constituted a whole novel!

"Take you to the hospital then?"

He shook his head, regretting it, as everything swashed about like a whirlwind.

"Just put me in a taxi, I must get home!"

That was the only thought in his mind, the relative safety of his secure accommodation.

"I can't let you go home in this state; I will come with you to see that you get there safely!"

With that she left him for a few moments, quickly returning with her coat and hand bag.

Fortunately, there were several taxis travelling along the busy road, and it only took her a few moments to hail one. It pulled over, and she opened the rear door, as Sagittarius almost fell in, and somehow she managed to get him safely inside.

"28 Lamborn Road."

That was all that he could manage, and although his location was secret, on this occasion he felt as though he had little choice but to reveal it.

Gemini held onto him as the black taxi cab pushed its way through the busy traffic. There she was again, right place right time, yet another coincidence!

It seemed like an eternity before they arrived, and when the taxi eventually pulled over to the side of the road, Gemini took some money out of her purse paying the driver, before slipping out into the busy street. The door opened and she helped him to his feet, legs buckling as he nearly fell, and she had to help him to steady himself.

Sagittarius lived in a pleasant tree line road, in one of the smarter districts of London, just off one of the main high streets. The houses were all nicely kept, mostly white washed and Edwardian, not too dissimilar to the clinic he had visited earlier. He instinctively reached for his keys, whilst trying to hold onto his raincoat and bag. He had left his umbrella at the clinic, but that was the least of his worries. Gemini had to help him as he nearly dropped them, and whilst she was helping him to put the main key into the keyhole, Oracle activated the security code of the hidden security system. It looked as though it was just a normal front door, but it was far from that. Sagittarius had installed the latest security systems, which

Oracle had control over, and its special array of sensors were something far beyond even those of the Department.

There was a clatter as he stumbled into the black and white tiled hallway, and he managed to grab hold of the coat stand as he steadied himself. This gave her time to close the door, and the locking mechanism clonked shut behind them. Instinctively, she took his raincoat off him, hanging it up, before placing his bag on the floor underneath. Taking hold of him, she helped him into the nearest room, which lay at the front of the house.

A real wood floor greeted them, a reproduction period feature like many within the house. Gemini's eyes bulged as she looked around; it was very smart, and tasteful with classic lines. Sagittarius gratefully dropped onto a designer couch, by a very elegant fireplace. The white marble reflected his dazed expression, as he struggled to maintain consciousness. Gemini sat next to him, feeling his brow which was giving off a lot of heat.

"Are you sure that I can't call you a doctor?"

He just mumbled *no* as the room whirred about as he struggled to focus.

"Can I get something for you?"

"Water."

That was all that he could manage to say.

Gemini left him, returning to the hallway, and following it to the end, where she found the kitchen. It too was very smart and elegant, beautifully fitted in a modern contemporary style. She could not help herself, and opened a few cupboards peering inside. Everything was immaculate, and again very tasteful.

Eventually she found a glass, and filled it from the tap of the purification system. She really liked this house, as it looked as though it had just come out of a glossy magazine.

Sagittarius liked his home comforts, and it had taken him several years to bring the old house back up to standard. His cover was that of a *Harley Street* doctor, and none of the neighbours took the slightest interest in him, which was just the way he liked it.

"There you are."

Gemini handed him the glass, which he nearly dropped, and she had to help him with it.

"Thank you, you are very kind."

She smiled, taking it off him and placing it on a coaster on a nearby table.

Meanwhile, Oracle had released the emergency catch of the escape panel of the bag, and hopped out, whiskers twitching. His sensors had been following Gemini and he had been analysing her. He needed more information, and so hopped along to the front room, where he could see them both sitting there.

She nearly jumped out of her proverbial *skin*, as he jumped right up onto her lap.

"Oh, how cute, is he your pet bunny?"

Sagittarius nodded, he was far more than a pet bunny, in fact, far more than she could ever imagine.

Oracle licked her hand with his rough tongue, depositing a good dose of nano robots in his saliva. She stroked his ears as the nano robots crept through her skin and into her blood

35

stream. She was totally oblivious, thinking that he was a real creature, and just being affectionate.

He then hopped onto Sagittarius's lap, and as he placed his fingers under his jaw, Oracle pierced his skin with his two needle like front teeth, one extracting a sample, whilst the other flooded his blood system with more nano robots. He then settled down, appearing to be going to sleep, whilst his processors went to work, analysing the sample.

Gemini gently stroked Sagittarius's forehead, running her fingers through his thick dark wavy hair, attempting to sooth his discomfort. She actually liked him, and his home, which was somewhat unfortunate. She now had mixed feelings, although her feelings were not entirely her own.

Sagittarius could feel her hands, which made him relax, although his mind was in turmoil. Memories were surfacing of all sorts of things which had been buried deep within his subconscious mind, as his body went numb. It was as though parts of his brain were separating themselves from the rest, and his mind itself was separating itself from his body.

His eyes were closed, and his limbs flaccid, as if they were not connected to him any more. Gemini waited for a while, still stroking his forehead gently, until she thought that he had lost consciousness altogether. Then she gently pulled back his eyelids checking his eyes for signs of activity. They just stared back at her lifelessly, which indicated to her that he was indeed unconscious.

When she thought it was safe to move, she got up, reaching for her hand bag, taking out her mobile telephone. Oracle was observing everything, still analysing the information. The outward impression was that of a pet rabbit sitting on his owner's lap, but inwardly his powerful processors were working overtime.

Gemini looked at him with regret, in another lifetime things could have been so different, but she had work to do. This was a dreadful business, and her conscience surfaced briefly, before being overruled.

Almost robot like, she left the room, heading for the kitchen to use her mobile telephone, briefly stopping to look back at him, before the urge to leave became too strong. There was conflict within her own mind, as two opposing forces slugged it out. One was a lot stronger than the other, and there was little that she could do to resist it. Resistance was one thing that Sagittarius also found difficult to do, as he felt himself slipping away.

Five

"Hello!"

"I have Sagittarius immobilised at his house."

"Excellent!"

"What should I do?"

"Stay where you are and I will send someone to you to take care of him."

The telephone receiver was placed down with a sigh of relief, mixed with one of satisfaction.

"Everything is going according to plan."

"Well thank goodness for that!"

"Yes, he had us all worried for a moment."

"If the doctor had not had the presence of mind to stick the needle in the back of his neck, it could all have worked out quite differently."

"Bit of a close call, that one!"

"We always knew that it was going to be a bit risky the way that he is, was!"

"Yes, he has always been a bit of a thorn in our side."

"Never liked the man."

"Me neither!"

"Bit of a maverick to say the least!"

"Brilliant mind though."

"That is the only reason that we put up with him."

"Well, we will not have to put up with him any longer, not that Sagittarius anyway!"

"Is the other one ready yet?"

"Should be in a few hours, when the download is complete."

"How is that going?"

"It seems to be progressing nicely."

"Then we should have access to whatever he has been up to."

"I hope so."

"So do I!"

"Well, we know that he has certainly been up to something!"

"Yes, we have had suspicions about him for a while, although he covered his tracks a little too well for us to have any definitive proof."

"Yes, just supposition."

"Hopefully we should soon have access to his private laboratory."

"Are you sure that he has one?"

"That sort always does."

"I wonder just what they will find when they get there?"

"Whatever it is that he has been secretly working on, the team will soon unravel it."

"We just have to wait for the new Sagittarius."

"I hope that he will be a lot easier to work with than the other one."

"I agree!"

"…and as for that dammed rabbit!"

On the other side of the city, Oracle had finished his analysis, and the results showed considerable contamination by the foreign nano robots. He was concerned, as even though he was what might be termed as an *Artificial Intelligence,* Sagittarius had been able to provide him with some limited emotions. This had proved to be very difficult, although Oracle did think the same thoughts as he did, being an extension to his own brain, and what might also be considered as his *alter ego.* His emotions were more like actions resulting from learnt behaviour, which are in essence the basis for all human emotion. It was a symbiosis between the two of them, and if there was going to be a loss of input or indeed purpose, then Oracle deemed that to be a threat, and would therefore take the appropriate action, and any action taken would be based on the results of his analysis.

Analysis summary

Subject: Sagittarius

Status: Critical

Prognosis: Subject showing signs of cognitive failure

Cause: Unidentified foreign nano robots detected in system

Action to be taken: Neutralise detected foreign nano robots

Method: Adapting and supplementing existing nano robots

Probability of success: 12.16%

Subject: Gemini

Status: Moderate

Prognosis: Subject showing signs of manipulation of neural cortex

Cause: Unidentified foreign nano robots detected in system

Action to be taken: Neutralise detected foreign nano robots

Method: Injecting modified nano robots into subjects blood system

Probability of success: 53.71%

Oracle's processor continued to run through the full report, whilst accessing how to modify his own store of nano robots to counter those that had been injected into both Sagittarius and Gemini.

It was basically down to their programming, as he carried a large amount of them which lay dormant within him. Each nano robot was only 0.5 micrometers in size, so small that they were impossible to see without the aid of a microscope. Looking like a miniature scorpion, each one was able to pack a considerable *punch*.

Sagittarius had a large amount of them within his body, monitoring his every function, constantly transmitting a wealth of information not only of his body but also his brain activity. It was the main way that they communicated, and Oracle used them to send information back, which was processed by Sagittarius's own brain.

Oracle had managed to slow the foreign nano robots down, and to block the transmission of certain sensitive information, but they had managed to compromise his system, and also to transmit quite a lot of information held within his brain.

The situation was very serious, as they had now placed him in a coma, and his metabolism had slowed down to such an extent that he was barely functioning. Oracle would have to ascertain the exact frequency that they used to transmit information, and also to reprogram his own nano robots to seek and destroy them.

It was very fortunate that he had been designed to engineer these molecular components, and reprogram his stock of *blanks*, which enabled him to constantly upgrade and replace any damaged ones. This task however, was going to stretch even his considerable processing power!

Sagittarius had originally designed them with working tools on their arms, and the transmitter in the tail. He would now, just like the real scorpions, have to add a *sting*.

His processor whirred in frenzy, concentrating on trying to block the foreign nano robots signals with the existing ones within Sagittarius's body, as well as programming the ones in his store to *seek and destroy*.

Gemini came back into the front room, her orders were to wait until the Organisation's representatives arrived, and she sat down next to Sagittarius with mixed emotions. There was also a battle going on within her mind too, as her conscience fought against the controlling influence of the nano robots. They were very powerful, and she had lost most of her own *free will*. It was a terrible situation to be in, and one which she had never asked for. No one volunteered to join the Organisation, they were just recruited, whether they liked it or not!

Her mind began to drift back several months, to a time long before she had been unknowingly recruited. How simple life had seemed, with just the ordinary worries of work and home to occupy her mind. There was now something else within it, a something that had already forced her to do several things which she would never have done voluntarily.

It had all started quite innocently, or so she had thought at the time. Back then she was plain ordinary Gemma Watson, with mousy brown hair, a plain ordinary girl who seldom wore makeup, and dressed very conservatively. Now she was peroxide Gemini, fully made up, and dressed provocatively. She had gone from a simple waitress, who was struggling to survive in the big city, to an Organisation operative with a task to perform.

The Organisation had invested their time and money in her transformation, and her whole personality had changed beyond recognition, and with a new identity, she was literally a new person!

It had been a normal day at the bistro, where she had been taking orders and serving customers as usual, when a rather shifty looking individual approached her stating that he was from *Head Office*. Apparently there had been a bit of an incident in one of the other branches and it was now company policy for all employees to have a *Tetanus* injection.

She noticed that he had a vacant look in his eyes, and was almost robot-like in his movements. Initially she assumed that he had some sort of medical condition himself, although she quickly realised that it was more like *radio control*. Her intuition spoke volumes to her, and she hesitated, her instinct had been against the whole idea, but she could not afford to

43

lose her job. So, very reluctantly she asked him to accompany her to the staff room.

The room was a little cramped with only the one table and four chairs, squeezed into the back of the bistro. He placed his bag down on the table producing some paperwork which she had to sign. It looked official, stating that it was to do with *Health and Safety*, and she had to sign, giving her consent. If she failed to do this, then as she suspected, she may well lose her job.

After the paperwork was completed, he produced a little bottle and a syringe in a new packet, which he opened whilst she was asked to roll up her sleeve. Gemini did as she was asked, and before she had time to think about it, he injected her in her arm. That was the moment that her life changed, as almost instantly she began to feel a little different. Luckily for her it was only a small dose, just big enough for them to be able to control her, but in no way as large as the dose which Sagittarius had been given.

Fortunately it had been near the end of her shift, and she had struggled on feeling a little dizzy. The rest of her day had been a complete blank, and she had awakened early the following morning lying fully clothed on her bed.

Gemini's tiny apartment, or more accurately *broom cupboard* as it was so small, greeted her, with the ceiling swirling as she struggled to get up. Everything seemed different, and she felt very odd.

For a start there was an envelope containing what amounted to several months' wages, and she wondered what she had done to acquire it?

Her head was swimming with all sorts of things, and several strange thoughts came flooding into her mind.

44

For a start she had the urge to take a week off, go to the hairdresser's and to be blonde, to have a complete make over, and to invest in some new clothes. For once, barely surviving on what she earned did not seem to matter any more, only becoming glamorous. That was the very moment that Gemini emerged, and her looks and personality were transformed. When she returned to work a week later, no one recognised her, and she had to admit that she barely recognised herself!

She had also been driven to find a man, not any ordinary man, but one in particular. This quickly became an obsession, and she could visualise him walking past the bistro, and she knew that whatever she did, she must not let him pass. She could see him in her thoughts, and then one day last month she had actually met him. It was as though she had been programmed to respond to him in a certain way, and her normally shy nature disappeared, and she found herself luring him into the bistro.

Little did she realise that it was the nano robots within her body controlling her thoughts and emotions. The Organisation had already transformed an innocent man in the same way that they had transformed her, and he was now waiting for a final download before undertaking his mission.

Today had been the climax of months of preparation, and she felt a sense of self satisfaction that events had conspired so that she was now sitting next to him in his home.

It was as though there was a voice inside her head telling her what to do, a voice so strong that it was difficult to resist. Now it was telling her to just sit there and wait, and as she sat there, her mind and body started to become numb.

Oracle had managed to access the frequency with which her nano robots operated, and everything she was remembering was being recorded by his processor. It was quite a story, and one which she had not the slightest clue she was sharing.

It was a picture of calm in the front room, and for the untrained eye it resembled a normal couple relaxing after a busy day. Who would have realised that they both had nano robots in their bodies which were controlling their very lives.

Sagittarius was slipping deeper into his coma, and Gemini was in a nano induced daze. There was no outward movement from Oracle either, although his processors were whirring round like a centrifuge. Estimates were that he was getting close to designing an upgrade to his own nano robots, and he was aware that the men from the Organisation would soon be pounding on the front door.

Having already established the frequency at which the foreign nano robots operated, which was slightly different for both Sagittarius and Gemini, he now needed to program the vast store of his own nano robots. The basic idea was to make them home in on the foreign robots, sting them with the scorpion tail so that it fried their circuits, and then to use the claws at the front to remove them so that they floated harmlessly into the blood stream, where their bodies would do the rest. Eventually they would work their way out and they would both be free of them.

Within his workings, Oracle had a self contained miniature laboratory where he was already experimenting. Each one of his nano robots had a little receiver and mini brain, so small that it was virtually impossible to see. Nano technology worked on such a minute level, that it required very sophisticated equipment. That equipment was held in Sagittarius's laboratory, which was something that had to be guarded at all costs. If ever the Organisation got access to the various projects within it, then there would be no stopping them!

Oracle was ready to start his first test, and he transmitted the computer code directly to a batch of his robots, and waited for the results. Initially there was a bit of confusion, and he realised that it was not going to be as easy as he originally thought. Oracle did have thoughts, which were more like reflections of Sagittarius's own thought patterns, which were stored within his memory.

The robots were able to communicate with each other, and they were also able to adapt themselves to any given task. It was not that they could not find the foreign robots, but that they only had limited power, which meant that just like a Bee, they only had the one sting. It was targeting that sting which was the main problem, as they had to strike a particular point on the foreign robots to *fry* their circuits.

The first batch had mixed results, until they adapted themselves by a process of trial and error, eventually learning where to strike. Results improved until they reached a level of 86.81%. In view of the impending arrival of the men from the Organisation, Oracle decided that he would have to settle for that, as time was running out.

He sent a signal to the remaining robots held in storage within his body, and when they were ready for release, he maneuvered himself, locating a vein in Sagittarius's wrist and jabbing his front teeth into it, injecting him with a large dose. There was no reaction at all, as he was still deep in a coma. Then Oracle moved himself round, nestling on Gemini's lap. She stirred slightly, as he located her arm, and she cried out when he injected the remaining robots into one of her veins.

47

Oracle sat there innocently, licking her, and she sat there in confusion wondering what had just taken place. She was still in a daze and could not work out whether it had just happened, or whether she was reliving the moment that she had been given her tetanus injection. She was still deep in reflection, going over and over everything that had happened to her over the past few months.

Oracle could do nothing more than to sit and monitor what was going on within their bodies, and hoped that he would be successful. Everything now rested on the battle which was raging within them, and with everything still in the balance, he could hear the sound of a large van pulling up outside.

Six

The rumble of the engine of an unmarked white van echoed along the tree lined road, mixed with the sound of other vehicles which trundled along between the neatly painted white houses. No one took the slightest bit of notice, as it pulled up outside number 28. It was a normal scene of any late afternoon, as the roads were always busy at this time of day, with commuters departing after their day's work and the rush hour beginning to gain momentum. Two large men wearing blue overalls emerged, walking casually to the rear of their vehicle where they pulled down the loading ramp, lowering it to the floor with a whirr of motors. The first man climbed onto it as the second raised it to door level, before sliding up the roller panel. Inside there was just one large cardboard box, and a tool bag.

They looked just like two ordinary men, about to deliver a large household appliance. However, they were not here to deliver anything today. Instead, they were here to take away the head of *Experimental Department*, who most people assumed was a doctor who worked at one of the London hospitals.

People went about their daily business totally oblivious as to what was actually going on, and as the first man slid the box out on a sack trolley, the second lowered the ramp again, until it hit the road surface with a dull thud. He then helped his colleague to roll it up onto the pavement, before returning for his tool kit. The normal everyday scene played out as they went to the front door, ringing the doorbell. However, what they were about to do was far from normal!

Oracle was the only one to stir, as Sagittarius was still in a coma, and having neutralised the nano robots in Gemini's system, she was in a state of total bewilderment. Her mind had begun to clear, and she now realised just what she had done, and what was about to happen. She had been part of a conspiracy, and one which had unwittingly formed quite a scenario. The Organisation was going to replace the head of the *Experimental Department* of British Intelligence, with an imposter, and one which not only looked like him, but also contained a lot of his memories. The process was now virtually complete, and the men outside were here to complete the task, with the removal of the Professor!

The door bell rang again with no answer, as Oracle hopped off the couch and through into the hallway. The door was reinforced with steel, and had been specially designed with a complex electronic locking mechanism. The windows were composed of bullet proof glass, and although this was extreme for any suburban house, security was one thing which Sagittarius took very seriously.

That was nothing compared to the basement laboratory which was more like a bunker, and somewhere that housed a lot of *cutting edge* technology. If that was to fall into the wrong hands then there would be very serious consequences!

The men tried to force the door, but there was no way they were going to get past the solid steel inner, and after a few moments one of them returned to the van to get further instructions.

"Hello."

"The door won't open!"

"Well, you will just have to force it!"

The line went dead.

"They are having trouble gaining access."

"Well, surely they know how to open a door!"

There was frustration in the Gentlemen's Club, which was shared by the man who returned to the house a few minutes later with orders to break in, although that was going to be easier said than done!

The dead lock was stubborn, and there seemed to be a series of interconnecting bolts, which seemed to be connected to some sort of electronic mechanism. Putting their shoulders to it, they felt the weight of the steel panel, and although they had a variety of tools with them, it was far more complicated than they had expected.

They could not just simply blow the door off its hinges with plastic explosives either, as that would have attracted a lot of unwanted attention. The windows also seemed very secure, and they cursed, deciding to see if there was a rear entrance. Unfortunately for them, the small rear garden backed onto the garden of the property behind, as the two sets of smart terraced houses ran parallel, with no other access points. So, reluctantly, they had no choice but to return the large cardboard box to the van and call for further instructions.

"Hello."

"It is very secure, with a dead lock, and bolts which seemed to be controlled by some sort of an electronic device."

"Wait there."

"There seems to be an elaborate security system in place."

"Most unfortunate."

"Yes."

"Do you think Gemini has been compromised?"

"I doubt it, but we will issue her with fresh instructions. Tell them to wait."

"Will it affect the operation?"

"No, just a minor set back. Once they get access they can neutralise the pair of them!"

"Good!"

"Those little chaps inside her will not let us down."

"What about the other Sagittarius?"

"He has received the update, and is on his way as we speak."

"Splendid!"

The other Sagittarius was indeed on his way, and had already passed the bistro and was heading towards the Tailor's shop in the up market arcade. His mind was now full of a vast amount of new information, and he was about to move into the next phase of his mission.

The shop was still quiet, which was perfect, as he had ordered a black pinstriped suit, white shirt, red paisley cravat, as well as a Gladstone bag. It did not take him long for the fitting and within half an hour he was ready to pass through the concealed doorway into the corridor which led to the Intelligence building.

Neither the Tailor nor his assistant noticed anything out of the ordinary, only the fact that for once in his life Sagittarius was dressed a little differently. He had emerged from the shop a few hours earlier dressed in his usual black pinstriped suit, and white shirt. Initially they had found this confusing, but his explanation seemed plausible, if not a little out of character.

The other Sagittarius had explained that he had been working undercover for a few hours, and had taken the opportunity to have his suit dry cleaned. He had purchased the grey suit from an ordinary gentleman's clothes shop as it did not warrant the expenditure of a Savile Row Tailors. This explanation seemed to suffice, as they were part of the *Secret Service* themselves, and used to undercover work. They held a variety of undercover clothing, and being as there had been a series of cutbacks naturally assumed that the department had now authorized some external purchases. Standards were slipping since the *Cold War* days, and nothing was as it used to be.

The other Sagittarius approached the retina scanner, which was hidden in a mirror placed on the wall of the changing room. It had been there for some time and was one of the older models. He looked into the mirror waiting for recognition, and there was a brief pause, before there was a subtle bleep. The scanner had failed to recognise him, and he tried again, as the nano robots tweaked his retina, causing his eyes to water slightly. This time there was a click, as the wall panel opened slightly. The nano robots had managed to fool the antiquated system, and with a slight push, he opened the panel, and slipped inside.

The corridor was dull and grey, and after a few moments the door clicked shut, leaving him alone in what seemed to be an endless tunnel. He had already been programmed as to where to go, and without a thought of his own, he walked calmly along towards the entrance to the main building. On his arrival he was greeted by another antiquated retina scanner, which looked well used. This time he was instantly recognised, as the nano robots had perfected their assimilation of the real Brandon Sagittarius.

The open door revealed a stairway, and he knew that the department head's office lay at the very top. It did not take him long to reach the solid wooden door, or to pass the final retina scan. Now he had access to all of the secrets held within the Experimental Department.

Within a few moments he was standing outside another large dark wooden door, and this one was marked with a nameplate;

EXPERIMENTAL DEPT HEAD

PROFESSOR B SAGITTARIUS

It opened slowly as he calmly walked inside the small room, with its solid oak desk and hat stand. The solitary green metal filing cabinet and two chairs, one either side of the desk made up the remainder of the furniture. On the desk sat a traditional green desk lamp, and various other small items of desk equipment. However, it was the laptop computer which held all of his interest, not to mention the secrets which he was after. He took no time at all in firing it up, and the only thing preventing him from accessing them was the encryption code.

The nano robots searched for the code, trying to access the real Sagittarius's brain via the other nano robots which had attached themselves to his cerebral cortex. Being as the human brain is somewhat similar to a computer, having a frequency that all thoughts, and bodily functions are centred around, it was a case of accessing the correct one, separating it from the multiple simultaneous frequencies which interact with each other to serve the various biological functions.

It was easy enough to analyse the extended low frequency range which they existed in, and indeed manipulate them to control his actions to force him to do what they wished. It was however, proving more difficult than expected as his own nano robots were busily counteracting the signals.

There was a brief pause, as all of the various frequencies were analysed, until the information from the real Sagittarius's brain was passed onto the other Sagittarius, revealing the password.

INCORRECT

This was typical of Sagittarius as whenever the wrong password is entered into a computer there is always a message displayed which says 'the password is incorrect'.

Now the computer could reveal all of its secrets, and he quickly slotted a memory stick into it, ready to download all of the information held on the hard drive.

All of the internal computers within the department were not networked, and ran on a closed system, to prevent any hacker gaining access. However, now that access had been gained it revealed several projects under development. Due to the present cutbacks there were less than expected, but the ones that were there the Organisation had a very keen interest in.

Project Creepy Crawley - small robot flies or wasps that could spy on individuals transmitting visual and audio signals, as well as a mini sting which could inject someone with several possible substances.

Project Bloodhound - an advanced tracking device, which could locate anything which contained a miniature tracking device, evading all of the latest countermeasures.

Project Papyrus - a plastic paper able to receive information like micro thin mobile telephone, which could only be accessed via biometric verification.

This particular project was of the greatest interest to the Organisation, as it meant that an individual's brain wave activities were measured via a simple repetitive test, and once recorded, they could be used to provide the ultimate security system as everyone has a different cognitive way of remembering something. Once the codes were accessed then the nano robots could duplicate them and there would be nothing that they could not gain access too. Sagittarius was the key, as they had already become aware of the research taking place, and targeting him would unlock everything they wished to get their hands on.

The memory stick flashed as the information travelled into it, and within a few minutes all of the information was there.

The other Sagittarius removed it, placed it in his pocket, closed the computer down and headed for the door.

The top floor was very quiet, and he slipped unnoticed back into the stairwell, before descending to the door at the bottom. The corridor was also deserted, and it took him no time at all to reach the Tailor's shop. Once inside, with nothing more than a brief nod, he was out into the arcade, mingling with the innocent shoppers, as he made his way towards 28 Lamborn Road.

Seven

The house was still and quiet, apart from the subdued noise of passing traffic, and the ticking of a large wall clock, which counted down the minutes before the other Sagittarius arrived. Outside in the unmarked white van, the men sat patiently waiting, studying their mirrors, and trying not to look conspicuous.

Inside, Oracle sat motionless, just like his two companions, as he monitored the battle taking place within their bodies. According to his readings, the friendly side was gaining the upper hand, although the hostile side kept on adapting and changing their behaviour, as the micro war waged on relentlessly, with both sides taking heavy losses. It was proving just as difficult to incapacitate the hostile nano robots as it was to remove them from where they had embedded themselves in the cerebral cortex of their victims, and it was proving to be a slow process. Time was running out however, as a black taxi cab pulled up at the end of the road.

Stepping out in his new clothes, the other Sagittarius paid the taxi driver and casually walked along towards number 28, playing out a scene which had occurred on countless occasions. The real Sagittarius always arrived home in a taxi, which was one of the little luxuries his generous salary could afford. Today however, unbeknown to the outside world, things were a lot different!

The two men noticed him approaching from the van's side mirrors, and climbed out to greet him. It looked as if they had been waiting to make a delivery and the occupier had now arrived. A passer-by looked briefly in their direction as she walked by oblivious to what they were actually doing. To her it was perfectly normal, and she was so wrapped up in her own thoughts, that she did not even grant them a second thought.

The door bell rang, and Oracle jumped down, hopping across the wooden floor into the hallway. There was no answer, as the other Sagittarius stood with the two men between the ornate terracotta plant pots, each containing a tall slim conifer, which stood on either side of the door. There was no reply, and so he looked into the retina scanner hidden in the brass door knocker, placing his hand on the brass door knob that sat in the centre of the solid black wooden door. There was a click, as the nano robots managed to confuse the security system, and the door began to open.

Oracle stared up at the glass panel above the door, which had the number 28 inscribed upon it in white numbering, as more light poured into the hallway as the door swung open. It was a shame that the new biometric verification system was still in the development stage, and if they had left it for another few weeks, then Sagittarius would have had time to install a prototype.

All three men walked in, and Oracle waited until they were clear of the doorway before raising himself onto his hind legs. The men stared at him wondering what a rabbit was doing in the hallway, but before they had a chance to think about it, Oracle shot a taser pulse out of one of his front paws, sending the other Sagittarius crashing to the ground. Everything happened so quickly that before they realised what was going on, he had successfully tasered all of them, and all three men lay in a heap on the floor as the door closed behind them.

Oracle had been busily calibrating just the right charge, and the bursts of electricity had not only temporarily paralysed them, they had also caused havoc with the nano robots within their systems. The pulse wave continued to reverberate around their bodies as he turned and hopped back into the front room.

The commotion disturbed Gemini, bringing her back to reality, and for the first time in months, her head was beginning to clear. She had many conflicting memories of things that she thought she had done, and other things which she thought she might have done. It was difficult to connect the two, as somehow she felt as though she was two different people. The usually shy girl was still there, although she felt the presence of someone else, who seemed to have a lot more self confidence. Opening her eyes, she could see a strange room and wondered where she was. Nothing seemed to make any sense to her and staggering to her feet, she wobbled slightly as she tried to regain her balance.

Memories began to flood back, patchy at first, but there was definitely something there. She could remember working in the bistro, and meeting the man she had been waiting to meet for what seemed like an eternity. Turning her head, she could see him lying on the couch, and he looked as though he was asleep. Obviously she must have made contact, and it looked as though she was in his home, which was very stylish with a contemporary feel to it. Still admiring it, and feeling a little groggy, she noticed a large mirror hanging on the wall above an ornate fireplace, and instinctively moved towards it.

What greeted her gave her a real shock, for there standing looking back at her was someone completely different. Gone was the straight mousey brown hair, replaced by peroxide curls. She wore full make-up and, as she looked in astonishment, there was a low cut top and push-up bra showing a very healthy cleavage. She also wore a short black skirt, and her legs looked tanned and healthy. She blushed, feeling embarrassed at the way she was dressed, although she had to admit that the transformation did make her look very attractive.

Other memories began to surface, as Gemini remembered a little more about how she had made the transition, and what she was doing in this strange house. Everything was still very hazy, with lots of broken and jumbled up memories. Remembering a little more about making the transformation and what she was doing here was one thing, but why she had done these things was something completely different!

The chime of the clock signalling the half hour made her jump, and she looked round; there lying unconscious on the floor of the hallway she could see three strange men.

"Aaaahhhh!"

She screamed, and her whole body went numb.

What had she done?

All kinds of thoughts entered her mind.

What had she become involved in?

Was she a burglar, had she become involved in some sort of a drugs gang, or even worse become a call girl?

Gemini felt sick at the thought!

All she could do was to stand there, and as she looked out into the hallway the front door began to open.

"Aaaaahhhh!"

She screamed again, as someone else entered the house.

She froze, in utter disbelief, for there standing in front of her was her twin sister Kate!

"What have you done?"

Kate pointed to the men lying on the floor.

"When I got your call I dropped everything and rushed over as you sounded very odd, and now I can see why!"

Gemini shrugged her shoulders.

"I don't remember!"

She then began to sob as her sister stepped over the bodies towards her, and they embraced, as she felt the safety of her sisters arms wrapped around her.

"What a mess!"

There seemed to be bodies everywhere and she had not got the faintest idea of who they were. Everything felt very strange, as if she was in some sort of a dream. She hardly recognised herself, and what made things even stranger, was the fact that she could not remember anything about her sister either!

They did look identical, even down to the peroxide hair. Their clothes were the same too, and she struggled to control herself in a state of total and utter confusion.

They parted, and as she looked back towards the couch, she realised that she did not know anything about the man lying there either.

Who was he?

Gemini struggled to find the answer to that question, and all of the others floating around in her mind. He did look professional, and handsome, and she had to admit that in his black pinstripe suit he looked quite debonair too. For some reason she felt drawn to him, and had the urge to join him on the couch, and so, sitting down next to him, she felt for a pulse.

He was alive, so at least that meant that she could avoid at least one count of murder!

She then began to wonder about the other men in the hallway. Perhaps they were still alive too?

If they were, then the situation was not quite as bad as it had first appeared!

Her momentary relief did not last long though, as a few moments later Kate suddenly pulled a taser gun out of her handbag, pointing it directly at her.

"What are you doing?"

Gemini was shocked.

"Following orders!"

Kate replied, her facial features suddenly changing from those of a compassionate sister to those of an assassin.

Before she knew what was happening, an electric charge shot out of the gun, making her whole body tingle, quickly followed by a searing pain, as if every molecule was being vibrated all at the same time. She felt paralysed, and then, just before she lost consciousness, she suddenly realised something.

She did not have a sister!

Eight

A shimmering haze engulfed Sagittarius as his blurred vision began to clear. His mind was awash with all sorts of memories, some clear, others very patchy. It had been quite a day, and he could not be sure of anything that his mind was telling him. Had he been to the Department today, or had he been working from home, and simply dozed off to sleep on his couch?

All he knew for certain was that his head ached, and his body felt as though it had been encased in concrete. Work had been stressful lately, with a lot of projects to manage, as well as the ones he had been secretly working on himself. Maybe it had all just caught up with him?

He closed his eyes for a moment, and when he opened them again he saw an attractive, provocatively dressed young woman standing pointing a taser gun at him. His instincts were to dive out of the way before she fired, although his body had other ideas, refusing to move. His eyes opened widely, and just as he thought he was about to be shot with a bolt of electricity, she fell to the ground. Oracle was standing on his hind legs in the doorway, and he could see the small cables retracting into one of his front paws.

All he could do was to stare in amazement at his creation, which had saved him from a very unpleasant experience. Oracle was truly remarkable, and over the next few minutes he was about to realise just how remarkable he really was!

Information was now flooding into his mind, as Oracle brought him up to date on what had transpired. It was unbelievable, and yet Oracle was not capable of telling lies, or making up stories. He just analysed information and gave solutions to problems. Sagittarius had to admit that he had gained his own personality, which was something that he had not even considered when designing him. Not quite emotions, but something akin to them. He was very loyal, and they thought the same way about everything, as he had shared so many experiences with him. Maybe it was learnt behaviour, or coming to the very same conclusions about most things, but whatever it was, he would be eternally grateful for everything that he had done.

The three men still lay on the floor of the hallway, and there were two women, one sitting next to him, and one lying on the floor at his feet. The both looked identical, and as he rose unsteadily to his feet, he also noticed that one of the men looked exactly like him.

Twice two!

He remembered the quote about everyone having a *doppelgänger*, but to have two different people each having identical versions of themselves in the same place at the same time was something that would only happen at a gathering of identical twins. Something was seriously amiss!

Sagittarius felt the need to sit down again, as Oracle came hopping into the room and up onto his lap. He then waited for further instructions, as he thought of what he was going to do next.

The clock ticked away until the hour sounded, bringing another quote into his mind, *For whom the bell tolls*. There was definitely something very sinister going on, and he needed to do something about it. Sagittarius was just a scientist, and an eccentric one at that. This situation called for a *secret agent*, and although he worked for MI6, this was way out of his realm of expertise. Everything was compartmentalised, and due to the secrecy involved, it was all carried out on a *need to know* basis. He would not even know a secret agent if he saw one!

Oracle assured him that the men would remain unconscious, so hopping off his lap, Sagittarius followed him into the hallway. Two of them were dressed in plain overalls, and looked just like they had come out of the boxing ring. They were tough looking individuals, with shaven heads, and pugilist features. They were both heavily set, and he struggled to roll them into the recovery position, checking their pockets as he did so. The only things that he found on the first man were a set of keys and two cheap disposable mobile phones. However, the other man proved to be far more interesting.

Somehow he had acquired Sagittarius's security identification, as well as several other interesting items, none more so than a computer memory stick. He also rolled him into the recovery position before gathering up the items and heading back into the front room.

Gemini had begun to recover from the effects of the taser, and although her limbs were still tingling, she managed to open her eyes, and could see an exact duplicate of herself lying on the floor in front of her.

"I don't understand!"

The taser had shocked her memory back into life, and it quickly cleared, revealing most of the things that had transpired earlier today, and over the previous few months as well. It was a lot to take in, particularly as she had now begun to fear for her life. Gemini started to tremble, not knowing what to do, and was relieved to feel Oracle's warm body suddenly snuggle up beside her. She instinctively cuddled him like a teddy bear, not having the slightest idea that he was in fact a cyber rabbit!

Oracle scanned her body with his processor to make sure that the foreign nano robots had been neutralised, whilst Sagittarius stood over her waiting for the all clear.

When it arrived, Oracle stepped aside and hopped towards the other Gemini. Now armed with a lot more information about the foreign nano robots, he injected her with the last of his own supply, waiting for them to take effect.

Sagittarius stood in disbelief, it had certainly been the strangest day of his life, and there was something very odd going on to say the least. It was a very complicated situation, and one that required a great deal of thought. For a start, it seemed as though security had been compromised within the Department, and his initial thought was to report it to someone higher up. However, he could not be certain who else had been compromised. Something had to be done, and he felt well and truly out of his depth.

Gemini smiled at him, although it was only a half smile, she looked very confused and worried too. A few tears started to flow as her emotions spilled over. She felt very vulnerable, having remembered a lot of things which had happened to her over the past few months. She also felt very guilty, having played a part in all of this. Sagittarius seemed such a nice man, and by the looks of things, he was about to be replaced. What would have happened to him, or her for that matter, if things had gone according to plan?

She shuddered nervously, before getting up, and putting her arms around him, hugging him gently.

"I am so sorry for all that I have done."

The tears flowed uncontrollably as she sobbed onto his shoulder.

"Well, what is done is done, and I know that you had little choice in the matter."

He knew that something very sinister was going on and that he would have to act, and decisively at that!

He held her in his arms, as his mind worked through all the possible scenarios. Whoever it was behind all this, knew where they were, and when the men failed to report in, then they would no doubt send others to finish off the job. Obviously they could not stay here, and as a mobile telephone rang, he suddenly realised that they would have to move, and quickly too!

Sagittarius eased himself out of Gemini's arms, walking calmly towards the men, although he felt anything but calm, but he knew that he would have to hold himself together. Stepping over them, he reached the front door, and there on the doorstep was a large cardboard box on a sack trolley. Without a moment's hesitation, he brought it inside, closing the door firmly behind him. The box had a front opening, and was obviously meant as a means of removing him. However, he could use this to his advantage, and after checking that the first man was still unconscious, he bundled him inside as best he could.

It was not easy as the man was quite large, but he managed. The plan was to get them all into the back of their van, and lock them inside. Sagittarius was very glad of the lift at the back, and it took him several minutes to get the first one safely inside. He also found some wrist restraints, and some material he could use as a gag, again obviously meant for him!

Finally after a great deal of effort, he had the three of them bound and gagged in the back of their van, and locked it securely before returning to his home. When he closed the door behind him he found that the other Gemini had regained consciousness. She was also very distressed, but he had no time to question her. Gemini was doing her best to comfort her, and he left them to it, as he picked up Oracle, and headed towards his laboratory.

The laboratory door was hidden behind a hinged book case, not the most original of disguises, but the best he could think of at the time. Sagittarius had never dreamed of being in such a situation, if he had, then he would have thought of something else. He seldom had visitors, and just wanted something discreet.

The book case swung open as he placed his hand over the secret panel, which recognised his fingerprints. This again was something which he had intended to replace with the new biometric verification system, when it was fully operational. Oracle activated the locking system, transmitting his code, and the large steel door clicked open revealing a flight of steps leading down towards the basement.

The laboratory was not very big, and lit by a series of bright halogen lights. It consisted of a raised worktop, which ran most of the way around the walls. The first thing that he did was to place one of Oracle's back paws on the recharging plate. It was only small, but very efficient, as he was able to recharge himself in less than ten minutes, and one charge would last for several days. Whilst he was doing that, Sagittarius pulled out a large black suitcase from under the work top. He had known that there would be the possibility that he would have to move his laboratory at some point, but never under these circumstances. All his equipment had been designed to fit neatly inside, and there was already a duplicate set of power cables in one of the pockets. He unclipped the adapter of his lap top computer, placing it carefully in its pre-prepared compartment, followed by a microscope, Oracle's repair kit, and the other specially designed pieces of equipment. There were also several vials of blank nano robots, and he was grateful of his foresight. Sagittarius took one of them, slipping a needle onto it, as Oracle opened his mouth. Just inside, there was a receptor, and he injected them into Oracle's nano store. Looking at the clock, he quickly closed the case, waited a few moments until he was fully charged, before grabbing Oracle with one hand, and the suitcase with another.

Sagittarius quickly climbed the steps, shutting both the steel door and the book case behind him. There was no time to go upstairs and grab any clothes, they would have to move very quickly, for he suspected that they were running out of time.

"We must go, now!"

Gemini looked at him, as her *doppelgänger* regained a little more consciousness. There was no time for any explanation, and whilst Sagittarius carefully placed Oracle back in his Gladstone bag, she helped her to her feet. She was very unsteady, but Gemini managed to get her to the front door, and within a few moments they were all standing on the front step. Sagittarius pulled the door shut, and they all moved onto the pavement, passing the white van as they went.

Although Lamborn Road was a relatively quiet suburban street, it was used as a cut through for the taxi cabs and rush hour traffic, as it avoided the mayhem of the busy main road which ran parallel. This had always been a real blessing, as it was easy to hail one, and fortunately today was no exception. A black cab was just passing by, and Sagittarius managed to get the driver's attention, and he dutifully pulled over.

"Paddington station please."

He opened the rear door, helping Gemini in with her *doppelgänger,* and the taxi driver released the boot catch, enabling him to open, and haul the suitcase inside. Within a few moments he was sitting next to Gemini as the taxi moved off. It was not a moment to soon, as just as they pulled out of the end of the road, a black Mercedes came screeching round the corner. Sagittarius looked out of the rear window as it came to a halt outside his house.

Nine

Silence gripped the black taxi cab as it forced its way through the busy London traffic, with no one wanting to say anything, which was just as well, as they were not certain whether the taxi driver was genuine or not. In fact, they were not certain of anything any more!

How many other people were involved in this conspiracy?

One thing was for certain, they would all be glad when they arrived at the station.

It seemed to take forever to reach the familiar glass and steel arch that marked the entrance, and when they finally arrived, it was with a great sense of relief that the taxi cab ground to a halt. Sagittarius climbed out, helping Gemini with her still recovering *doppelgänger*. She looked bewildered, and got a very strange look from the taxi driver.

"My sister is unwell."

He seemed to be reassured by Gemini's comment, and gratefully accepted the rather exorbitant fee. There was little choice, and it was a good job that Sagittarius had a generous salary. He liked to pay for everything in cash, and keep himself as anonymous as possible, even using a disposable mobile telephone, registered to a fake name and location. It was just as well, as he now realised that whoever was behind all of this had already gathered quite a lot of information about him, not to mention the Department. They needed to get away, so that he could do some investigating of his own, and there was only one place that he felt safe, and it certainly was not in London.

With one hand holding his Gladstone bag, and the other his suitcase, he led the way, as both of the Gemini's followed on behind, as they pushed their way through the crowd. Normally these days, most people book their tickets online, but it would be cash and no questions asked for them!

The booking clerk was surprisingly cheerful, a little too cheerful for Sagittarius's liking, raising his eyebrows as he looked at the two very attractive young women with him. Sagittarius remained cool, although underneath he was a little flustered.

"Three for Bristol Temple Meads please."

Sagittarius handed over the money, and the clerk directed them towards the correct platform. They were in luck as the train was already at the platform, and due to depart in just over ten minutes, which would give them time to settle in. After boarding, Sagittarius helped his two companions to their seats, and stored the suitcase before taking one of the seats opposite. They were travelling first class, as it would give them some well needed privacy, and they all breathed out a huge sigh of relief when the doors began to close, and the train readied itself to depart.

Oracle sat in his Gladstone bag on the seat next to Sagittarius, scanning the compartment and studying the other people inside. It was almost empty, with the only other occupants being a group of Oriental businessmen. They were engrossed in some sort of construction project, and had a set of plans draped over the table in front of them. Oracle signalled that it was safe to talk, and it was now time to find out just why there was a duplicate of the real Gemini and more importantly, who she really was, and what she was doing here?

Her name was Caprice Parker, and she was of a similar age to Gemini. They both had a similar build, and he could see that it would not have taken much effort to make them look alike. She worked in a clothes boutique, and he could now see where they acquired their outfits. Caprice had been approached in a similar way to Gemini, only this time she had been taken into the INNER VISION Private Health Clinic and Cosmetic Surgery, where Doctor Crawley had performed some face altering procedures.

Sagittarius had trouble hiding his own facial expressions, as not only had another innocent girl had her life changed without consent, but it also meant that his own *doppelgänger* had been recruited and altered by the very same people. The more that he learnt about what had been going on, the more worried he became, and his feelings only increased when he found out her code name *Caprica*.

It was no coincidence that they all shared astrological names, and being as there were only twelve star signs, then that meant that it would be fair to assume that there were another nine people involved in this conspiracy. He slipped his hand into his pocket and pulled out the mobile phone he had taken from one of the men. He had been very bullish, and it came as no surprise to find out from the information stored within it that his code name was *Taurus*. The other man was more of a mystery, and from the text message carelessly left undeleted, he was code named *Aquarius*.

The plot had indeed thickened, and as information from Oracle flashed up on the inside of his dark glasses, his thoughts began to drift back to the telephone conversation earlier today that had started all of this.

It was obvious that the two men, whom he had instinctively placed in a Gentleman's Club, were the ring leaders, which he doubted were the real heads of this organisation. Little did he

73

realise just how far reaching the Organisation really was. So, the three of them, plus the two men who he had left bound and gagged, and locked in their own van made it five, and the two in the club made it seven. It was therefore logical to assume that they would be encountering at least another five individuals at some point. It was also worth noting that they were obviously after information about the secret projects, and other research held within the Department, to which he was key. The main questions were what they intended to do with it, and more importantly, what exactly was this organisation really up to?

The more he thought about it, the more alarming the answer became. Just how many people had been affected by the nano robots, and just how far did this organisation reach?

Oracle's processors whirred as he thought the same thoughts. How many people in authority had already been compromised?

What they needed was a way of detecting the nano robots. More information flashed up on the inside of Sagittarius's glasses, indicating that Oracle was working on the problem. It was going to take him some time, and whilst he was busily working, Sagittarius decided to spend a little time with his companions.

He took his dark glasses off, resting them on his knee as he studied the womem. It was extraordinary how they had been made to look almost exactly the same, with only a slight difference, and one which unless you studied them closely, you could barely tell them apart. For a start, there was the peroxide blonde hair, and each had the same shade and style, with what looked like a light perm. The hair was just past shoulder length, with both of them having quite heavy make up, which made them look very attractive. Being slim and standing around five feet eight inches in height, they both had curvy figures, and ample cleavages which poked out of their half unbuttoned black blouses. They both wore short black skirts, and black shoes with a high heel which extenuated their shapely legs. Looking at them, he had to admit that they were both really beautiful women.

Sagittarius was a single man, married to his work, and one who had dabbled with relationships in the past, but had never quite found the right person to form a long lasting relationship with. He was a handsome man in his own right, smart and intelligent, and although he had received some female attention, he had calmly brushed it aside. Now sitting opposite two real beauties, his mind did begin to wonder for a moment!

Both women were in their early to mid twenties, and being as he was probably old enough to be their fathers, he dismissed the thought. However, from the seats opposite, the same thought was being contemplated. They were looking at him, wondering if he might be interested in them?

His handsome, slightly tanned features, swept back black wavy hair, combined with his muscular physique, and being over six feet tall, ticked several of their proverbial boxes. He was also very smart, and uniquely stylish, not to mention having a healthy salary and his own contemporary house on the smart side of town. They both smiled at him warmly like a pair of sirens, each thinking the same thought.

Oracle, who was sitting quietly in his Gladstone bag, had thoughts of his own, still calculating busily, as well as sending an urgent email from a secure, untraceable account. He was confident that both Gemini and Caprica were now free from control, and the message flashed up on the inside of

Sagittarius's dark glasses. He noticed it, as well as the message confirming the next part of their plan.

Now that he had received the *all clear*, Sagittarius decided that he was going to take the unusual step of sharing some personal information with them. After all, they were both victims of this situation, and at the very least deserved some sort of an explanation. So, clearing his throat, and making sure that no one was able to eavesdrop on their conversation, he shared some of what he knew. His explanation did not involve revealing Oracle's true nature, or his equipment, as that would have been a step too far!

The young women had mixed emotions as he told them what had happened, and they shared their experiences with him too. In some ways it was very cathartic for them, and in other ways very distressing. They both felt guilty that their actions had nearly resulted in his capture, and no doubt interrogation, with or without the nano robots. Also, having informed them that he worked for the Department, questions of National Security arose. All in all, it was just like the plot for an espionage movie, although when the seriousness of the situation dawned on them, it became a little too real!

Their conversation died as the guard appeared checking tickets, and Sagittarius watched him ogling his female companions as he handed over the three small pieces of cream coloured card with the red orange edges. The guard studied them, and the two very attractive young women, who noticing his unwarranted attention, uncrossed and crossed their shapely legs in unison.

He blushed slightly, and when he had seen enough, he handed them back to Sagittarius with a big grin on his face. He had obviously made up his own story of why they were here, and little did he know what was actually going on. When he was out of earshot, the two women smiled at each other, somehow seeing the irony of the situation, before they resumed their conversation.

Time seemed to rush by, just like the countryside, and their journey of just short of two hours seemed to fly by, and it was with real surprise that the guard's announcement over the intercom informing them that they were approaching Temple Meads station, broke their conversation.

The two young women looked at each other, and then back towards Sagittarius. What were they going to do in Bristol?

Ten

The stone façade of Temple Meads station stood resplendent in the late afternoon sunshine, its carved features and delicate designs giving testament to the master craftsmen who created it all those years ago. It was a surviving relic from a grander age, sitting in complete contrast to the battered old Land Rover which pulled up outside, its paintwork flaking, revealing the aluminium body underneath. It was already getting late in the day, and fortunately it was not quite as busy as it had been earlier, and so the driver was able to pull into one of the vacant parking spaces. Opening the door, he slipped down onto the tarmac and headed towards the pay and display meter. Hopefully he would not be here long, as he hated big cities, and was eager to get back to the countryside. Once he purchased his ticket, and stuck it on the windscreen, he closed the door with a heavy *clunk*, before heading into the station.

A screech of metal wheels on the steel rails signalled the approach to the station, as the train wobbled slightly as it moved over the points. It was time to get up and make their way towards the exit, and so Sagittarius grabbed hold of his Gladstone bag, reaching for his suitcase, as the two women held onto their matching black handbags.

Other passengers did the same, and as the train ground to a halt, there was the usual disorderly scrum for the exit. Gone were the days of good manners and etiquette, being replaced by selfishness and self obsession. Sagittarius was however *old school*, and had impeccable manners, allowing the crowd past him, as he waited patiently for his turn. He gestured for the two women to go first, and they waited patiently in the doorway as he stepped down onto the platform. Then placing his suitcase on the slabbed edge, he offered his hand first to Gemini, and then to Caprica as he helped them both down from the train.

They both smiled warmly at him, appreciating his good manners, and secretly they both desired him, even though their thoughts were focussed mainly on their situation, and what they were doing in Bristol.

The bustling crowd headed towards the exit, and Sagittarius observed them, looking for anyone suspicious. He had been careful not to give any indication of where they were going, although he could not be quite sure if they had been followed, or whoever was behind this conspiracy had not sent someone to meet them. However, there was one person who was waiting for them, and as they got to the outskirts of the station, a man walked forward to greet them.

He had a bushy greying beard, and long greying hair, which poked out of an Australian styled hat - minus the corks. He wore a denim jacket, jeans and a paisley shirt and had on a pair of Chelsea boots. He stood over six feet in height, and had a large muscular build, looking like a cross between an *all in wrestler* and an ageing *hippie*.

The two women were amazed as Sagittarius dropped his suitcase, putting his arms around the big man, giving him a hug.

"Nice to see you dad."

The big man reciprocated

"And you son."

They continued to embrace for a few moments, and when they parted, the man looked at the two women who were accompanying his son, winking at them.

"I can see that you are doing very well for yourself these days!"

For the first time Sagittarius blushed, and the two women smiled back at him.

"This is Gemini and Caprica, but I have no time to explain."

"You have not got to explain anything to me son, whatever makes you happy!"

Sagittarius blushed again, much to the amusement of the two women.

"Can we get out of here?"

He changed the subject quickly, before his father could say anything else.

"You will have no objections from me. Oh, and by the way, I am James Justice Joplin Sagittarius, although everyone calls me Big Jim."

He gave Gemini and then Caprica big bear hugs, lifting them both up off the ground.

"I am so glad that *Brand* has got himself fixed up at last."

Parents always have a way of making their children squirm, and for Sagittarius, his father's comments made him feel very uncomfortable.

"Wait till I tell your mother!"

Both women laughed, secretly wishing that it was true. They instantly liked Big Jim, who was a very charismatic figure and a man in very good shape for his age. Jim was in his early sixties, and looked as if he had just come from *Woodstock*.

"I've parked outside."

He pointed toward the car park, and without further ado, they followed him out of the station.

His Land Rover was the traditional green colour, looking almost military, and when they approached he unlocked the back door, easily hauling Sagittarius's suitcase inside. Sagittarius helped the two women up into the back seats, before climbing in next to his father.

Starting the engine, he pulled away.

"So, tell me what brings you here?"

Sagittarius shared everything that had happened with his father, who nodded periodically, as they made their way out of Bristol, down the A39. They were heading for Glastonbury, where his parent's had a smallholding on the outskirts of the town.

The journey took just over an hour, which gave him plenty of time to fill his father in on the details, and it was quite a story!

The Land Rover pulled off the main road, heading down a country lane which stretched deep into the countryside. It was such a contrast to the hustle and bustle of London, with not a soul about apart from one passing car. Sagittarius's father waved at the occupants, and they waved back. Everyone knew Big Jim, as he was very popular with the locals, even if some of them thought that he was a little on the eccentric side. His eccentricities were not just limited to the way that he dressed, but also to his beliefs, which were something that the two young women were going to have to get used to!

Big Jim lived an *alternative lifestyle*, and was one of those people who were at odds with most of society, and what was about to unfold was going to make him seem far more rational than people ever gave him credit for!

The Land Rover pulled up over a small hill, as the hedge lined road stretched out into the countryside. It was not far now, and Sagittarius began to relax as he knew that he would soon be back in familiar surroundings. He always liked to return to his parent's house, and was a regular visitor, although he knew that whoever it was that was behind all of this would also know. It was inevitable that they would receive some uninvited guests, but at least it would give him some valuable time, and his parents would be able to give them some valuable assistance.

"Here we are!"

Big Jim announced proudly, as he turned off the road and the Land Rover rumbled over a cattle grid as it passed through a set of gates and into a long driveway. That was the only feature that marked it out from the rolling countryside, apart from a small red post box and a wooden sign.

FREEDOM FARM

The driveway stretched out before them, delving behind a hillock which obscured its view from the entranceway. The two young women looked out of the side windows, trying to see the farm, although there was nothing to suggest that there was a farm here at all, apart from the sign. In fact, it looked just like an ordinary field in the middle of nowhere, as the whole place was deserted. The driveway began to curve as they approached the hillock, and as they turned away from the road, they spotted something just visible in the distance between the bushes and clumps of tall grass. They were not quite sure what they saw at first, but as the drive veered round, what greeted them was what appeared to be a subterranean dwelling.

All the buildings were hidden from sight, and it was not until they were almost on top of them that they could see the whole farm, tucked into the hillside. It comprised of a hillock, with the centre hollowed out, and the buildings forming a circle around what appeared to be a paved courtyard. The drive ended just before the hillock, by a half submerged garage, and the two young women gasped as they looked at the farmstead.

It was the first time that they had seen anything quite like it, and as Big Jim beamed with pride he brought the Land Rover to a halt.

"Welcome to my home."

Both men slipped out of the vehicle, opening the rear doors, and helping them down, as they stared in amazement at the curve of buildings all painted white and dressed with an adornment of glass.

"It took several years to complete, but it is a real eco house - a bit of a bunker really!"

The farm was certainly something, and looked as eccentric as Big Jim, although having said that, it was also as smart as Sagittarius, with everything so neat and tidy. There was a garage, greenhouses, and lots of rooms all peering out of the hillside towards them. The driveway ended with a small gravel path which led up the side of the hillock and down into the courtyard.

The side of the hillock was just about high enough to give the courtyard shelter from the prevailing wind, and it was not until they had reached the top that they had a full view of the buildings. They followed the men down the slope, and as they neared the edge of the stone paving, one of the large glass doors opened and out walked a very attractive woman with long flowing blonde hair.

"Welcome home son."

She put her arms around Sagittarius giving him a big kiss on the cheek, and an even bigger hug.

"Who have you brought with you?"

She slackened her grip on him, as he introduced his travelling companions.

"I would like you to meet Gemini and Caprica."

Sagittarius's mother removed her arms from him, placing them first around Gemini and then Caprica.

"I am so pleased to meet you, and I am Astrid, Brandon's mother.

They were a little shocked as she looked far too young to be his mother, although she was actually nearly sixty.

"It's the yoga and healthy living."

She could sense the surprise at her youthful looks.

"That is more than can be said for me!"

Big Jim smiled broadly, and they all laughed with him.

"Come inside, and tell me all about yourselves."

They all followed her in through the glass door, and found themselves in a large kitchen.

"I bet you are thirsty, and a little hungry after your journey."

She was not wrong, as none of them had had anything to eat or drink for hours.

Gemini and Caprica sat down on two of the dining chairs which sat around a large wooden table.

"What would you like to drink?"

She offered them a choice of all sorts of things, informing them that she only drank water. They could see that from her complexion, that it had been doing her a power of good. Astrid also offered them some of her organic biscuits, which she had made earlier, and the two young women felt instantly at home with her warm and affectionate nature.

In the meantime, the men left them to chat, returning to the Land Rover, to retrieve the suitcase and Gladstone bag. On their return, they disappeared into another of the buildings.

Big Jim was a computer scientist, and had been working with computers since the seventies. He knew practically all there was to know about them, and had been instrumental in Sagittarius's education. He had also played quite a part in the creation of Oracle and knew all about nano robotics, and cybernetics. Most of his work had been done for the big multinationals, and although he hated them, they had rewarded him generously. Now in semi retirement, he made his living doing consultancy work, and working on his own projects too. It might seem that he was a respectable company man, but that was far from the case. Big Jim was a radical thinker, and had many conspiracy theories. However, just like his son, his employers had little choice but to contract him as there was no one else who had his particular set of abilities.

"So, they have finally caught up with you!"

Sagittarius sighed, his father had been right as usual.

"You realise that they will he here soon."

It was Big Jim's turn to sigh.

"I have been expecting something like this to happen, and it was only a matter of time…"

They had to act fast, and Oracle downloaded all of his information into Big Jim's computer, while he scanned through it muttering to himself as he picked his way through the technical stuff.

"Very clever, but not quite clever enough!"

Sagittarius looked a little more optimistic, even though he seldom showed his true emotions, and it was obvious to his father that all of this had really got to him.

"It's a good job that they have not got hold of your research, as it would have closed a lot of the loopholes they have left for us to exploit."

Silence descended as Big Jim pulled on his beard, deep in thought.

Meanwhile, in the kitchen Astrid was busily entertaining her guests.

"So, how did you meet my son?"

Gemini and Caprica both took a deep breath, and together they began to explain all that had happened to them. It was quite a story, and the more they spoke, the more alike they seemed to become. Although they were not related, even though they looked almost identical, they were becoming *one*. It was uncanny how similar they were in personality, with their voices merging too. Maybe it was the nano robots at work, but whatever it was, it was as though they were *clones*.

Astrid smiled periodically, realising that they had both started to develop quite a crush on her son. Again, the foreign nano robots had been programmed for them to form an attachment to him, to gain his trust so that they could pass on vital information about him. Now that they had been nullified, for the most part, it was their true personalities that had begun to surface. Astrid smiled to herself, she had been waiting for a long time for Brandon to bring a young lady home to meet his parents, and now he had brought two!

It was quite an amusing situation, and the more she thought about it, the more she realised that there would be difficulty in separating them from him. She knew her son very well, and realised that he had not the slightest idea what was going on. He was very good on the technical stuff, but when it came to relationships, it was another matter!

Astrid liked both of them, and the more they spoke, the more she realised that they were now speaking together, using the exact same words like two *peas* in the proverbial pod.

"It sounds as though you have had quite a day!"

Gemini and Caprica smiled at her, realising that they had been talking for quite some time. Astrid had a lot of patience - she had too, living with Big Jim!

"Would you like me to show you around?"

The two young women had almost forgotten that they were in a very unusual house, and jumped at the chance to have a look around.

Freedom Farm was an extraordinary place, and one which Big Jim had created with the help of some trusted friends, and the proceeds of some very lucrative contracts. Astrid had designed the interiors, and the courtyard. She had a love of flowers, and had excellent tastes, being very artistic. Astrid and Big Jim were like one, although different, their complementary opposites fitted together like a proverbial glove. They had been together for years, and were affectionately know as the *odd couple* by their friends.

Astrid took a deep breath, before explaining more about their home.

"Jim designed the farm, and got the idea from being stuck behind a milk lorry of all things. I'm sure that you have seen them with the big tank on the back. Well, Jim thought that you could connect them together - a bit like a submarine. So, he designed a system of interlocking tanks, which could be buried in the ground. They are cast in one piece with an oil layer between the inner and outer shell. They are coupled together in a horse shoe, with windows into the courtyard and light tubes placed in the roof of the corridor, which runs around the inside, giving us plenty of additional light. Jim wanted it to be as eco friendly as possible, so they are cast from recycled plastic and form a tough polycarbonate shell. It was quite exciting seeing the hole dug out, filled with gravel and then the shells placed on sand, which is good for drainage. Then sand was placed around the rest of the shell, then more gravel, before the soil and then the whole thing was grassed over. It was my job to design the interiors."

Gemini and Caprica looked in wonder, not realising that a subterranean house could be so light and airy, and pleasantly warm too.

"The floor, wall and ceiling panels were fitted to the shell which gave me a wonderful blank canvas to play with. There are no radiators to worry about, as all pipes and cables are hidden behind the walls. The whole thing went up in only a few weeks."

It was certainly revolutionary, and Astrid could see that they were a little confused as to where the heat was coming from.

"Everything is heated by what Jim calls a *Ground source*. Heat pumps use pipes which are buried in the surrounding land to extract heat from the ground. This heat is then used to heat the oil within the layer of the shell, as well as providing hot water. According to Jim, heat from the ground is absorbed into the fluid and then passes through a *heat exchanger* into a *heat pump*. The ground stays at a fairly constant temperature under the surface, so the heat pump can be used throughout the year - even in the middle of winter."

There was no need to put the lights on as they entered the corridor, and Astrid went on to explain a little more about her very unusual home.

"We also have solar panels which provide us with all of the electricity that we need, and we have a well too for our water, reed beds to purify the waste water, and we even grow our own food, so we are virtually self sufficient!"

"Wow! The two young women spoke together, and thought that the whole complex was fabulous. They could do nothing but look in wonder at the lounge, and bedrooms, and there was also plenty of storage space too. Their tour led them round to the greenhouse, where most of their food was grown, and eventually they ended up in Big Jim's laboratory, where he was still busily working through things with Sagittarius.

"Hello there!"

Big Jim greeted them with a big warm smile.

"We love your home!"

Gemini and Caprica both spoke together, smiling back at him.

"It's a little different, but so are we!"

He began to laugh, enjoying the fact that their creation had met with approval. Everyone began to relax, although they knew that it would not be long before they had to deal with some uninvited guests...

Eleven

The Gentleman's Club was a grade one listed building with its stone columns and black painted iron railings, that stood as a bastion to sophistication and the lost days of empire. It was a *men only* establishment for the *well to do*, with membership only granted to those of power and influence. Situated in one of London's more *upmarket* areas, it offered confidentiality, and a place where secret business meetings could take place, as well as discreet conversation for those who had the wealth to afford membership. It also offered *other* services to those who required a *certain something!*

Today, the requirements of two of its members had more than one sinister connotation, as a telephone call was received giving an update on their ongoing operation...

"What!"

"They have escaped!"

"How has this happened!"

"They found the other Sagittarius, Taurus and Aquarius bound up in their own van!"

"Well, it is no use trying to break into the house now, as they would have already removed everything we wished to acquire before they made their getaway."

"It appears that Sagittarius is far more resourceful than we gave him credit for. Somehow he has been able to counteract the nano robots, and what makes it worse is that he has taken the memory stick containing all of his research. This is not good, not good at all!"

"Where could they have gone?"

"I would not mind betting that they have headed to his father's."

"So, at least we know where they will be. Can we send a team to pick them up?"

"It will not be as easy as that."

"Why not?"

"His parents live in a bunker."

"Bunker?"

"Yes, a subterranean dwelling that will prove difficult to enter."

"Bit like a mole then."

"Far worse!"

"How?"

"Well, his father who they refer to as *Big Jim,* is also a scientist - very clever sort of a chap. It runs in the family!"

"How clever?"

"He is one the world's leading experts in nano robotics, and cybernetics."

"Well, getting hold of his research should more than compensate for the loss of Sagittarius's, and maybe we can recover his information too. Sort of killing two birds with one stone!"

"It might be possible."

"Surely they will not be able to put up much resistance, they are only scientists after all!"

"You may well be right, but the situation is a little more complicated than that."

"How do you mean?"

"Well, he is one of those *tin foil hats.*'

"*Tin-foil hats*, what on earth is one of those?"

"A conspiracy theorist."

"Thinks that there is a secret organisation trying to take over the world."

"How ridiculous."

"Yes I know!"

"He obviously knows too much."

"Maybe we should have been more discreet."

"We have discredited him as we have all the others, although potentially he could blow the lid off the whole thing."

"Maybe we should silence him. After all, it would not be the first time."

"Yes, but we must get hold of his research first."

"It could prove quite messy, particularly as he has worked for military intelligence in the past, just like his father before him."

"Well, we do have a certain influence within both the British and American military, and others around the world too. We are part of a global operation after all!"

"The plan was to keep it simple, and just remove Sagittarius, we will have to get authorisation from the committee."

"Sounds complicated."

"Yes."

"They may have to move their plans forward."

"Well, seems as though we have little choice."

"I will have to make the call…"

There was a brief uncomfortable pause in the discreet corner of the Gentleman's Club as both occupants of the *chesterfield* chairs looked at each other in trepidation. They knew only too well that making the call would put them at risk. The Organisation liked everything to run according to plan, and any deviation met with more than just a sense of disapproval. They were ruthless to the point that if they did not get their own way, then heads would roll - literally!

"Hello Arachnid, this is Scorpio, and I have Aries with me. I am sorry to bother you, but we have a problem with Sagittarius."

"Yes."

"Taurus and Aquarius were found bound in their van, and Sagittarius has escaped with Gemini and Caprica."

"We are not pleased!"

"Can I have authority to send the others after them?"

"Do you know where they are?

"We suspect that they have gone to his parent's home."

"Well you will have to deal with it, and tidy everything up as we do not wish to have any loose ends, and use a good cover story. The last thing we need is to draw attention to ourselves."

"Yes, Sir."

"You have twenty four hours, and use everything at your disposal."

"Yes, Sir."

"We cannot accept failure, I will contact the committee, and if you fail, well you know the consequences."

"Yes, Sir."

The colour drained out of the face of the man holding the telephone receiver as the line went dead.

"Well, what did he say?"

The other man looked equally worried, as he waited for the answer to his question.

"We have twenty four hours."

"Then what?"

He knew what the answer would be, although he was hoping against it.

"We will be dealt with ourselves…"

Big Jim's laboratory was quite something, containing various pieces of exotic computerised equipment, and various other custom made items, which were just as unique as he was. His research had taken him way beyond his initial hope of helping those who had lost a limb, or suffered severe nerve damage. By tapping into the brain's neuronet, he had found a way of triggering a response in an artificial limb, and also found a way of accessing those parts of the body which had become paralysed by various accidents or conditions. He was a very compassionate man, whose official working career had ended

95

several years ago, although now he was making great strides in cybernetics and nano technology.

To the untrained eye, he was nothing more than a software technician, although those who understood exactly what he was doing would have been astounded at the progress that he had made. It was one thing to try and bridge the link between an artificial limb and the brain, and quite another to have designed a cybernetic intelligence. Sagittarius had been able to provide various classified items of research, not to mention make his own contributions, and there, sitting on the work top, was their greatest creation - Oracle.

Neither Gemini nor Caprica had the slightest idea that he was a *cyber rabbit* and not just a pet bunny. They naturally assumed that being animal lovers, Oracle was just part of the family. He was, although he was far more than that!

Oracle had a very powerful processor, which was linked to Big Jim's even more powerful computerised system, and not only that, but he was also able to control ten other cyber rabbits. They all sat quietly on a padded dog bed at the far side of the laboratory, each looking identical to the other. The room seemed to be full of black rabbits, a sight which amused the two women.

Big Jim was eccentric, still stuck in those far off hippie days of his youth, never having got over his belief in love and peace. Astrid was also very hippieish, teaching yoga and practising many forms of alternative medicine. It had seemed like a good idea at the time changing their surnames to Sagittarius, and adding a few extra middle names to complete the ensemble. Astrid Star-child Sagittarius, and James, Justice, Joplin, Sagittarius, to be precise. Little did they know that their choice of surname would one day provide the cover names for some of the Organisation's operatives!

Calling their son *Brandon* had also seemed like a good idea at the time, as they had both been reading a book by *Brandon S Centerwall*, who had written about the *Green Man*. They had been fascinated by the spirit of the forest, and had read that the name also meant *little prince*, and *brush covered hill*, which was where he was conceived!

Sagittarius was dreading his parents telling that story, and was relieved that his parents were going to spare him the embarrassment. He had got used to the name *Brandon*, although everyone just called him *Sagittarius*.

It also seemed as though the two young women had been stuck with the names *Gemini* and *Caprica*, and in an odd sort of a way they suited them. They were so alike, and being as Gemini is renowned for being twins, it seemed appropriate. Maybe they both should have been called Gemini, but there had to be some way of telling them apart.

They both looked at him in a *certain way*, and even though it made him feel uncomfortable, Sagittarius had to acknowledge that they both had what appeared to be quite a *crush* on him. That was another problem that he would have to deal with, although it could wait until they had dealt with whatever they would have to face next. For some reason, he had always felt a little uneasy around women, even though he had always received a lot of love and affection from his parents. Life had made him a bit of a loner, and working for the Department with all of its restrictions, he had found it difficult making friends. After all, with all of the secrecy involved, and his research, allowing a woman into his life would have caused him all sorts of problems.

Big Jim sat down on a chair in front of his large computer screen, and by the way he was sitting it looked as though he wanted to have a serious talk. Astrid noticed the signs, so after exchanging brief pleasantries, she took the two young women away with her, even though she got the distinct impression that they wanted to remain close to her son.

"I have processed the information held within Oracle's main processor, and reveal some rather interesting results."

Sagittarius waited with anticipation, as his father's years of experience were about to be revealed.

"What I have discovered is that the nano robots implanted into both of the girls in particular have yielded a fascinating residual effect."

Big Jim looked very pleased with himself, as if what he had discovered had confirmed something that he had suspected for quite some time.

"Nano robotics offers the possibility of many great leaps forward in medical procedures, and as you know I spent many years trying to help those with nerve damage, and others who struggled to control artificial limbs. The main problem was getting the brain to interact with other parts of the body, or indeed any replacement items."

He thoughtfully ran his index finger and thumb over his bushy beard.

"The brain fires neuro impulses to the muscles via neuro pathways to tell them what to do, and when there is a break in the chain, the limb remains still as it fails to receive its orders. In some other cases the limbs seem to have minds of their own, as they only get a partial message. In effect it is an *on and off*

98

switch. Nano robots, if calibrated correctly can bridge that gap, taking the messages from the brain and directly transmitting them to the appropriate muscles."

Sagittarius nodded.

"That was the main purpose of my research, and I was making progress until I discovered that there were alternative uses."

Sagittarius thought about what had happened to them, understanding a little more about why his father took early retirement. He loved his father, although he had to admit that even to him his behaviour was a little *too* eccentric at times.

"Not only do they offer the possibility of being injected into the body to make repairs, such as a damaged or partially blocked artery, heart valve, or to destroy a tumour without external surgery, but they also open up the possibility for missuse, such as brain control!"

Sagittarius nodded again, realising where this was going.

"There were some companies who were keen to exploit this possibility, and when I found out what they had in mind, I decided it was time to leave. They dismissed me as a fool, an old hippie who had finally *lost the plot* so to speak. However, I knew as well as they did that it was only a matter of time before somebody, somewhere, discovered just how to manipulate the mind for sinister purposes."

Sagittarius spoke for the first time in ages.

"Well, I know from first hand experience just what it feels like!"

Big Jim nodded, still stroking his beard.

"It's always strange how these things happen, and the universe often presents us with opportunities, and not always good ones!"

They looked at each other, as Sagittarius readied himself for what was to come next.

"When the brain has been altered, it is never quite the same again. I know that Oracle has managed to neutralise the effect of the nano robots within your system, and those of the girls, but they have left a residual trace - a *Ghost in the machine!*"

Sagittarius looked worried.

"A *ghost* is something which we are aware of but unable to make contact with on the physical plane, which is unaffected by material barriers. It is invisible to all but those few with psychic abilities or those able, if only for a brief moment, to sense other planes and dimensions."

Sagittarius thought about his mother. Astrid was one such person, and could have made a living out of being a *medium*, although she used her *intuition* when prescribing alternative medicine. She just had a *knowing* about things, and he had grown up receiving messages from his grandparents and other family members who had passed away. He was so used to it, that it had become part of daily life, and even though they were not with him in person, they had always been with him in *spirit*. It was no wonder with his mother's abilities, combined with his father's expertise, that everyone referred to them as the *odd couple*. Glastonbury was one of the only places where they were truly accepted, as it was renowned as being the psychic capital of the country. Having said that, his parents were eccentric even by Glastonbury's standards!

100

"A *ghost* is the dissolving fragment of a life left after the body has ceased to be, after all nothing ever really dies. Take a candle for instance. When the wick burns down into the wax, you get smoke and heat. It is the same with a human being. The achievements, hopes and fears, beliefs and memories live on as energy - consciousness. Now the universe is one big consciousness, and whatever you call *God*, the *Creator of all that is,* or any other term you care to use, it is one big thinking organism. It exists, and as it experiences, it evolves. Nature is a learning experience, and the planet is covered with fossils of extinct species. Some have died out due to climatic change, or been hunted to extinction by various predators such as man. Those that survive have to change or die - evolution if you like. No matter how small the creatures, somewhere within them is consciousness."

The conversation was getting very deep, although Sagittarius was used to his father, and was interested to find out just where all of this was leading.

"Just like a radio or television program or a piece of music, when it is transmitted it continues to travel out into the universe. There could be an alien listening to the first playing of *Piece of my Heart* right now - he was a big Janice Joplin fan after all!"

Sagittarius thought back to those wild early days in the VW Camper van, travelling from festival to festival, whilst his parents relived their hippie trail days - it was certainly a different sort of childhood!

"It is just the same with conscious thought, as consciousness creates, and thought turns in to matter. Jerry Ragovoy and Bert Berns thoughts manifested in the song *Piece of my Heart,* which they created out of their consciousness, manifesting it into matter, which was then released back into consciousness via the radio waves."

Big Jim paused for a moment, reminiscing.

"Our thoughts are very similar, and the electrical field which once constituted the ego of a man, his individual awareness, also continues to exist. What we have here are the electrical impulses of the frequencies used to transmit the signals to the nano robots injected into you and the girls, combined with the residual electric field which they have left."

Sagittarius looked at the graphs displayed on the screen.

"This line here, shows the range in which we would expect to find normal thought, and this one shows us what the nano robots transmit."

There was clearly a difference. Big Jim was a genius just like his grandfather, and although Sagittarius was a very clever man, he had nowhere near their brilliance. He often wondered how his grandfather had been able to help crack the Enigma code, which was thought to be impossible. In those days they did not have the advanced computer technology available today, with most of the work being done by the brain.

"Oracle was able to isolate the exact frequency used and to jam it, whilst programming his own nano robots to seek and destroy the foreign nano robots. However, they have had a lasting effect upon you all."

Sagittarius looked worried.

"For a start, you are a little less confident than you were, and you must admit they have had an effect on your personality, even though you were only exposed to them for a relatively short period of time."

Now that his father had come to mention it, he had been acting a little out of character.

"The girls might have had their appearance altered on a physical level, but have you noticed how alike they have become on an emotional level too?"

His father was right, they both shared the same mannerisms, and when they spoke, they spoke together, being more like *one* than *two*.

Big Jim brought up some more information.

"I have figured out a way of not only blocking the frequency used by the nano robots, but also to detect their presence and more importantly, change their very programming…"

Twelve

The laboratory fell silent as Sagittarius took in all that his father had told him. He knew that his parents both held deep spiritual beliefs, not to mention a whole host of skills, gifts and talents. What his father had been saying did make perfect sense to him, and he was very grateful, if not relieved that he had made the right decision in coming here. He knew whoever was behind this would also realise where he had headed, and that it was only a matter of time before they arrived, probably in force. Big Jim was the only one he could turn to, and he hoped that together, they would be able to prevent them from getting their hands on their research.

"From what I can deduce, whoever is behind this has taken your astrological name, and used it as a code word. It is no coincidence that the two young women you have brought with you are called Gemini and Caprica."

Sagittarius had been thinking along the same lines, and took what his father was saying as confirmation.

"Now, as we know there are twelve signs of the zodiac, and having already used three, that leaves the remaining nine."

Big Jim changed the screen, revealing a list theorising who and what lay behind it.

"For a start, having that hunch that there were two people behind the original telephone conversation, and the fact that you thought they might be in one of those *Gentleman's Clubs* - you know that you have inherited certain of your mother's *gifts*."

He was right again!

"I would therefore suggest that they would probably use the code names of *Aries* - strong willed and a risk taker, and *Scorpio* - big and bold with a nasty sting in the tail. From what you also told me about the men who broke into your house with your *doppelgänger*, I would guess that their leader would be *Taurus* - strong and stubborn, with great stamina, accompanied by *Aquarius* - intelligent and rebellious. That doctor Crawley is likely to be *Pisces* - after all there was something fishy about him!"

Big Jim started to laugh at his own joke.

"Logically, that would leave us with *Cancer, Leo, Virgo,* and *Libra.*"

It all sounded perfectly logical despite the bad joke, and even if he had got the odd code name wrong, it was still very plausible.

"However, there is a thirteenth sign of the zodiac, one which is seldom used, *Arachnid* - spinning a web of intrigue, and ready to pounce on any unsuspecting soul who gets caught up in his plans. I would not mind betting that that is the person in overall charge!"

Again, he could not doubt his father.

"So, I would expect that before too long, we will be seeing everyone apart from Aries, Scorpio, Pisces and Arachnid."

He was right again, and there would probably be up to six uninvited guests appearing later that day, or early the next!

At least they now had a good working theory, and knew a little more about what they would be up against. There was still one question however, which he would like the answer too.

"How many copies do you think they have made of me?"

105

Big Jim smiled.

"Don't worry son, I doubt if they would have wasted any more resources on duplicates. The only reason they duplicated you once was so that they could gain access to your work, not to mention infiltrate the Department. They also needed a backup of Gemini, just in case anything went wrong with her, as she was your main contact, and it is doubtful whether your *doppelgänger* will be with them. He is probably waiting for you to be neutralised so that he can take your place!"

Sagittarius frowned, whatever relief he felt at the knowledge that there were only two of him disappeared at the prospect of him being *neutralised!*

That thought lingered on, grating at the pit of his stomach, and he was not the only one to feel his stomach trying to tell him something. Time had flown by, and they had been talking for over an hour. Big Jim was hungry, and although he lacked Astrid's psychic abilities, his stomach always knew when it was dinner time!

So, they left Oracle minding the proverbial *shop*, and headed back towards the kitchen, knowing that they had some serious programming to do later.

The sound of voices grew louder as Sagittarius followed his father down the corridor, as the smell of food being prepared brought a smile to Big Jim's face. Astrid was a very good cook, accounting for Big Jim's rather rotund figure, and tonight they were having a curry. Being vegetarians, there was obviously no meat, instead there was a home made pickle tray and poppadoms, nan bread and a wonderful biriyani, harping back to their hippie trail days across India.

"I knew you would appear when I was ready to dish up!"

Astrid laughed as Big Jim entered the room.

"Well you know me!"

She certainly did, Big Jim was one of those people who lived to eat as opposed to ate to live. Sagittarius was also looking forward to one of his mother's meals. There was nothing quite like her home cooking, which was one thing that he really missed living away in London.

Caprica and Gemini were very pleased to see them, smiling broadly as they entered the room.

The meal was glorious, and the conversation centred on their adventures. There was much laughter, which really helped to break the tension as Big Jim shared several stories, which Sagittarius knew off by heart. He was made to squirm by mention of his childhood, but the two young women loved every minute of it. They had been welcomed with open arms, and both shared the same thought, that whatever happened they were going to remain part of this family. It was obvious how they both felt about him, although the feeling was not reciprocated. One woman would have been acceptable, but two was overwhelming!

With the meal drawing to a close, Big Jim looked at the large clock which hung on the kitchen wall. They would have to leave soon and return to his laboratory, as there were preparations to be made. Somehow they both knew that before the night was over they would have received unwelcome guests.

So, after finishing off, they made their apologies and left the table to get stuck into their task. Big Jim already had a basic plan, and together they worked on it until they were ready.

"Right, send out the Lads!"

Oracle, transmitted his orders, and the stealth rabbits all obediently got up off the dog bed, and formed an orderly line. Then, they marched in unison towards the open door, heading for their designated positions.

On the main computer screen there was a map of the farm, with small numbered balls indicating their progress, as they fanned out taking up their allotted positions.

It seemed very odd having ten *stealth rabbits* as a form of self defence, but they were no ordinary rabbits, being cybernetic and full of all sorts of advance weaponry. When they were in position, their black fur acted as camouflage, making them almost impossible to detect. They then switched their eyes to night vision, and in the unlikely even that they would be detected, they would just appear to be ordinary rabbits lying in the grass waiting for the approaching dawn.

Big Jim threw a switch on the wall and the storm shutters automatically began to lower. Each door and window had one, as well as the sky lights, and everything now resembled a sealed bunker. The idea was quite simple; to protect the farm from everything but a direct hit, and even then there was still a good chance that they would survive. There was little prospect that they would be hit by an artillery shell, although he knew that if they managed to get past the *lads*, then they would still have to defend themselves. Everyone had been given a taser gun, which had enough power to knock out any intruder, and give them just enough time to bind their hands and feet. Real guns were out of the question as it went against their philosophy of *peace and love*. There would be little of that in the coming hours, as they all knew that the uninvited guests were here to apprehend them, or in the worst case scenario, eliminate them altogether!

Over the years, Big Jim had gained quite a lot of information about such groups as the Organisation, and although he did not have direct information about them, he knew that there was a global group who had operatives in many key locations. Their aim was to control the whole planet, and getting hold of Sagittarius's research, as well as having a mole in the Department would be another step towards their goal. He also knew that his research would be very dangerous if it fell into the wrong hands, which is why he had spent so many years in preparation.

Most people thought that he was losing his mind whenever he spoke about it, as conspiracy theorists are always dismissed as being paranoid and more than a little mad. Some information had already leaked out by those who were either brave or foolhardy enough to release it, and had been quickly discredited by the very people the information was aimed at. It was nothing short of a secret war, and in a climate such as this, it was difficult to know who to trust. Now, having gained an understanding of exactly how they were going about it, Big Jim had the vital frequencies with which their nano robots operated. He suspected that all members of the Organisation, and possibly the wider group had been injected with them, with a central command controlling their very minds. He also doubted if many of their number actually realised that they were being controlled, and the whole thing was a very complex and disturbing scenario.

It was no wonder that most people would not believe him, and there was no one else that he could call upon for assistance. It looked as though they were on their own, and he was glad that his son and his companions were with him. This day was inevitable, and he was very grateful that they had not decided to raid the farm sooner. The whole prospect had made him a little paranoid, which was one reason for designing the farm as something resembling a bunker.

Freedom Farm was isolated, which presented a bit of a double edged sword. On the one hand it did give them privacy, apart from the odd visitor, but on the other it made them vulnerable, as there was no one who would know that they were being attacked. Two black Land Rovers turned off the main road heading in their direction, and as the radar picked them up, all they could do was to wait, and hope that everything would go according to plan.

The kitchen was also quiet, with the three women periodically staring into the lap-top screen which sat on the large wooden table. They had also been briefed, and held onto their taser guns, ready to defend themselves if the need arose. It certainly was *quiet before the storm*, and the *tornado* would be here in only a matter of minutes.

The Land Rovers pulled into a small lay-by at the side of the lane, often used by walkers who would drive out here and follow one of the many footpaths that led all the way up to *Glastonbury Tor* which dominated the local landscape. It was a good walk from here, and most people approached it from different angles, but there were some who just liked to just enjoy the countryside. For the Land Rover's occupants, they had far more on their minds than an historic monument. Their orders were quite explicit, capture and eliminate all occupants of *Freedom Farm*, and recover all available research. So, battle lines had been drawn, and battle itself was just about to commence...

Thirteen

The faint flicker of light cascaded through the hedgerow, sending eerie shadows into the field before suddenly disappearing as both vehicles switched off their engines. Tonight was going to be a *special operation*, and one which they all knew could not end in failure. Their orders were quite explicit; recover all data and eliminate the occupants. Failure to do this or to make it look like an accident would have major repercussions, and repercussions within the Organisation were very serious indeed!

Big Jim was correct in his assumption, as there were indeed six of them. Taurus was their leader, and gave the signal as they all donned black balaclavas and readied themselves and their equipment for what was to come. Opening the doors, each man grabbed his back pack, along with his weapon, and lined up behind him. He was what could be described as a *bruiser*, bald, scarred and tattooed, thick set and muscular, and someone not to be *tangled* with. He had already failed once, and was determined not to fail again. That went for Aquarius too, who was not quite so well built, also having a shaven head, and a rather creepy, sneering grin. The others, who had the code names *Cancer, Leo, Virgo,* and *Libra,* were equally as unpleasant, and the nano robots within their bodies had already removed any sort of a conscience.

They were the nearest thing to human robots, devoid of any sort of emotion, apart that was from negative ones. They all wore black combat suits, complete with body armour, and carried an assortment of guns, all fitted with silencers. They almost looked like *special forces* personnel out on a training exercise, although on this occasion it was for real.

Taurus raised a finger, and they all followed him, keeping low behind the hedgerow, trying not to make the slightest noise. They had deliberately chosen the lay-by as it was out of sight, and being in the early hours, there was little chance of any passer-by noticing their vehicles. They were painted black, with false number plates, and when they returned they would remove all traces that they had ever been there.

Every man had been *recruited* from the army, and knew exactly what they were doing. *Stealth* was their middle name, and success was virtually assured.

The night was overcast and dull, providing perfect cover as they crept along. Daylight would be hours away, and when the dawn finally broke, they would be miles away. Everything was working like clockwork as they neared the gate, which was the only entrance in or out of *Freedom Farm*.

Cancer crouched by the gate post, giving cover to the others as they crept over the cattle grid with hardly a sound. He was just about to rise up and follow the others when he felt a sharp pain in the back of his leg. Reaching down, he pulled out a small dart, and as he examined it, he wondered where it had come from. To him, it looked like an air gun dart, with a sharp tip, small barrel and a tuft of black fibre. He signalled to Libra, who crept back, wondering what he wanted. He bent down, as Cancer showed him the dart, pointing to back of his leg.

He examined it, and whilst he was bending over, another dart was fired at them, and this one embedded itself in his backside. He nearly jumped out of his proverbial *skin* as he felt it penetrate his trousers. He pulled it out, showing it to Cancer, and they both looked round, trying to find out where the darts had come from.

Everything was quiet and there was not a soul about, apart from them. It was very odd, but when they received a signal from Taurus, they automatically crept over the cattle grid. Cancer found some cover behind a bush and stayed to guard the entrance, whilst Libra moved up to join the others, rubbing his backside as he went.

"Well done numbers one and two!"

Big Jim was delighted that the first two stealth rabbits had successfully hit their targets. Each rabbit carried a dart, which he fired from his mouth. The darts contain nano robots, programmed to infiltrate the men's bodies. It had taken a few hours to program them with the information Oracle had collated earlier. All they had to do was to wait, and they would gradually take over the intruders' systems.

His eyes were fixed on the screen, as he watched the others creeping along the driveway towards the main building. The men were totally unaware of what was going on, not expecting to encounter any resistance. Their orders were to break in and neutralise the inhabitants, download all relevant information, and destroy everything before they left. The cover story was going to be a fire, caused by an electrical fault. They had a man on the inside, the local Police Inspector, who was going to tidy up any loose ends.

The Organisation had many tentacles, and nothing was left to chance. This information was vitally important to them, and they were determined to recover it at any cost. If anyone caused them a problem, the Inspector carried a syringe, and would inject nano robots into them to bring them under control.

"We are receiving the first information from the nano robots."

Sagittarius looked a little surprised.

"That was quick!"

Big Jim briefly looked at his son.

"I made a few adjustments."

Cancer and Libra had no idea that there were now new nano robots within their bodies, nor the fact that there was now a battle taking place within them.

Taurus signalled for the men to fan out, and they ran around the perimeter of the hillock, forming a circle. Leo, a large muscular man with thick wavy hair crushed under his balaclava, took cover by a bush, which stuck out of the hillock. He was waiting for the signal to advance when he felt a sharp pain in his arm. Looking down he also noticed a dart, and pulled it out with disgust. In the bush he could see a pair of pale eyes staring at him, but as he swung his gun around, he felt his whole body tingle with electric charge. Number seven had hit him with a taser, which was concealed in his left paw, and before Leo could do anything, seven jumped out of the bush, and hopped away from the hillock as fast as his little legs could carry him. Leo could not move for a few moments, and when he did, seven was out of sight.

"Got another one!"

Big Jim made a mental note. Now half of the men had been injected, and no casualties so far.

Taurus crept up to the top of the hillock, using his night vision binoculars to examine the complex. Everything was in *lock down*, with storm shutters protecting all of the exits, as well as the windows. This was something that he did not expect, although he did carry some plastic explosive. He would have to blast his way inside, and it was fortunate that the farm lay in

114

the middle of nowhere. He doubted whether anyone would be able to quickly identify where the noise had come from, and when they eventually did, they would be long gone. He signalled to the others to join him in the courtyard, and they circled back round, leaving Leo as another lookout.

The storm shutters were quite thick, made of solid steel, but would be no match for the plastic explosive. He could see that there was no chance of prising them open, so took a clump of the plasticine like substance out of his jacket's left front pocket, placing it in the centre of the nearest shutter. He then pushed in the detonator, and took the small electric switch out of his right front pocket. The other men took cover, sheltering behind the large stone sculptures which formed the centre piece of the courtyard, whilst he climbed up the hillock.

"They are going to blow the storm shutter away from the kitchen, get out of there!"

The three women heard Big Jim's voice boom out of the walkie talkie, which was on the large wooden table, and grabbing it, along with their tasers, they ran into the hallway. It was not a moment too soon, as there was an explosion, followed by the sound of shattering glass and the clang of twisted metal, which rained down like hail on the courtyard slabs.

Virgo, another tough looking individual felt a sharp pain in his shin, and looked down, thinking that he might have been hit by a piece of shrapnel. But all he found was a dart, fired by number five, who had been hiding in a sculpture. It did not bother him, and he just pulled it out as he and the others rushed towards the opening.

"I'll go!"

Sagittarius grabbed his taser, leaving his father to go to the aid of his mother and the girls. Fortunately they were unharmed, although very shaken by the explosion. Taurus rushed in, followed by the others, who were able to squeeze their way through the hole in the storm shutter.

The kitchen was almost completely dark, with the only light coming from the hallway, which was just enough for them to see that there was no one inside. It was a complete shambles, with broken glass everywhere. The force of the explosion had shattered everything in its path, and the floor was littered with debris. It was a good job that the women had managed to get out when they did, as they could have been seriously injured.

The men crunched their way across the floor, passing a wrecked laptop computer, which was now lying on the floor with a cracked screen. Libra, the computer expert, grabbed hold of it, clearing space on the kitchen table before placing it down. It was completely dead, so he left it there, as there was no point wasting time trying to get any information out of it. He turned round to see Virgo crouching down by the doorway giving cover, as the rest of them burst through into the hallway.

It was deserted, as everyone had fled in the direction of the laboratory, which lay on the other side of the complex, passing Sagittarius as he went in the opposite direction. Although heavily outnumbered, and only lightly armed with a taser and an air pistol, he was determined to try and stop them.

The men advanced, bursting into the lounge, which was also deserted. They were going to go from room to room, and Sagittarius's desire to stop them looked hopeless. It was only going to be a matter of time before they made their way to the laboratory, and when they arrived, it was almost certain that they would be able to get what they wanted.

Sagittarius, had other ideas however. His tough uncompromising self returned as he took up a position in the doorway of one of the bedrooms. He could hear the men approaching, and as he crouched down, guns in hand, he saw a tell tale shadow. It was moving carefully along, and what looked like the barrel of a gun pointed in his direction. He readied himself, and as soon as he saw the tip he fired his taser. The wires shot out, striking the black metal.

A paralysing current of electricity shot along the barrel towards the hands grasping the gun, and there was a muffled cry followed by the thump of someone hitting the ground. The figure of a man dressed all in black rolled into sight, and Sagittarius quickly shot a dart out of the air gun, which caught the figure on top of the head. Time seemed to stand still, as he lay there with the little feathered dart sticking out like a small unicorn's horn. In a way it was quite amusing, although this was not the time, or the place, for humour.

Taurus felt his body go numb, not even noticing the dart sticking out of his head. The others halted, backing away slightly, wondering what had happened to him. This gave Sagittarius just enough time to back away, and to retract the wires, and prepare himself for the next encounter.

Taurus urged Aquarius forward, as he lay there, his body still suffering the effects of the taser. Aquarius crept forward, and just like Taurus, he felt the electric shock reverberating around his body, as he fell to the ground, a dart piercing the woollen material of his black balaclava too.

All six men had now been injected with nano robots, and Big Jim studied the readings on his computer screen. It was now up to Oracle to coordinate the nano robots, as Big Jim grabbed his taser and the women rushed into the laboratory. They were clearly shaken, and Jim signalled them to take cover behind him as he moved forward.

Back in the bedroom, Sagittarius lay in wait. He knew that he had to slow them down in order to give the nano robots a chance to take effect. He also knew that four of the men had already been injected, and that he had shot a dart into another two, although being as they were all dressed the same, he did not know whether he had got some of them twice.

Taurus was now almost fully recovered, and his temper was rising. He was very angry, and just like his namesake, he got to his feet and charged forwards past the others like a bull. Sagittarius shot him again, but not before he had managed to get off two shots with his rifle. The first one missed, hitting the door frame and splintering the wood, but the second caught Sagittarius in the shoulder, and he fell to the ground together with Taurus.

A sharp pain came from the wound, as blood poured out from beneath his suit's jacket. Fortunately it had missed the main arteries, but it was enough to send him temporarily into shock. Once again time seemed to stand still as the others rushed forward, standing over him with their guns trained upon him. There was nothing that he could do, and he dropped his weapons, now totally at their mercy.

Taurus got back to his feet, raising his gun to fire again at the helpless Sagittarius. He really wanted to kill him, but he was just about able to control his raging temper, realising that he needed information out of him first.

Big Jim could hear the scuffling, and knew that there was something wrong. He had taken up position near the laboratory doorway, and had thoughts of possibly barricading them inside, as it might just gain them some precious time. It was then that he made his decision.

"I'm going out. Close the door and push anything you can find against it, and whatever happens, don't let them inside!"

He was worried about his son, who he assumed would have returned shortly after the women. There was no sign of him, and he felt that he had to do something. So, he picked up his taser, and a white hand flare bought for an upcoming sailing holiday. He loved the feeling of the wind and the waves, and part-owned a small yacht with a group of friends. It was going to be their turn soon to take a few days break, and he had stocked up on some emergency supplies. Fortunately, he had the box ready in his laboratory, and he hoped that what he had in mind would work.

The women just obeyed him, as he was quite commanding when he wanted to be. So, without thinking, they just did as he said.

It all seemed surreal to them, as they pushed a filing cabinet, against the closed door, along with any other pieces of furniture that they could find.

For a moment, it harped back to the days when men were in charge and women did what they were told. Neither Big Jim nor Sagittarius were normally anything like that, and had always treated women as equals, and would have frowned on such behaviour. Astrid had always been an independent woman in her own right, running several small businesses, and she had always enjoyed a relationship based on equality and sharing. They got on so well together from the first time that they had met, and had seldom had an argument in the forty odd years that they had been together.

119

Big Jim was so easy to get along with, and charming and funny too, which was in contrast to most scientists. She gave him the time and space to do what he did, and plenty of support if he needed it. He always included her, and whenever he had a contract that meant that he would have to work away, she often accompanied him. Today however, he had kept the seriousness of the situation from her, hoping that somehow the men would not try and storm the farm. They had, and used plastic explosives too, and were now heading their way, heavily armed and determined to carry out their orders.

Gemini and Caprica were bewildered by everything, and although they were also independently minded, the shock of the explosion, combined with the realisation that they had been *controlled*, in some way, made them thankful that someone had taken charge.

The three of them stood on the far side of the laboratory facing the door, and as the cold realisation of what was happening began to sink in, they all began to wonder whether they would ever see Big Jim and Sagittarius again?

Big Jim slowed down, holding his taser in one hand and the flare in the other. For a big man he was very light on his feet, and the curve of the hallway gave him an advantage. Just like his son, he waited for the shadows on the wall, and just when the first one crept into view, he set off the flare, throwing it forward. The flare gave off a sudden bright light, dazzling the men and causing enough confusion for him to rush forward and fire his taser at the first one. Taurus dropped to the ground, and as he fired twice more in quick succession, Libra and Cancer also fell to the ground. The cartridge in the taser only gave him three shots, so he bowled into Aquarius knocking him to the ground.

120

There was quite a struggle as he tried to tie the men's hands together with some plastic straps that he used for keeping his papers together.

Big Jim managed to get them around Taurus's wrists, as he lay helpless on the ground, and Cancer's, before they regained some use in their limbs. He just about managed to tie Libra's hands together before he felt the butt of Aquarius's riffle on the back of his head, and he rolled over, unconscious on the floor.

Fourteen

A blinding pain throbbed through Big Jim's head as he tried to open his eyes. His vision was blurred and he had trouble seeing anything. His arms ached and his wrists were sore, as he realised that they were bound together with the very straps he had hoped to use on the men. They had also dragged him to the laboratory door, and next to him lay Sagittarius, also bound, and bleeding. The wound had caused a big red stain on his shirt, and there was also a bloody hole in his suit jacket. He looked very pale, and had lost quite a lot of blood.

Big Jim found it hard to focus, and still even harder to comprehend. He had been so close to securing the men, and now he lay dazed next to his son, who had been shot. Sagittarius was also barely conscious and he desperately wanted to go to his son's aid, but as he tried to move, he found that the bindings were tight, and he drifted in and out of consciousness.

It was as though the whole world was spinning, and the pain in his head would not go away. He was strong, even though his age was against him, and he fought against the feeling of drift. It was as though he was neither here nor there, or anywhere, as he kept slipping in and out of this nightmare situation.

Astrid had taught him the art of meditation, amongst other things, although this was not the time or place to relax and connect with his *Higher Self*. Having said that, though, he did start to concentrate on some breathing exercises, and as he filled and emptied his lungs, it began to help. The more oxygen he managed to get into his body, the more his senses began to return. He also tried to breathe away the pain, another technique which was really helping the situation.

122

After a few minutes he was able to focus properly, and there standing over him were four men, all dressed in black combat suits, with balaclavas hiding their faces. All he could see were four pairs of eyes staring down at him, each brandishing a gun, which they looked ready to use.

"We have the Professor and his father, and if you don't open the door, then we will shoot them both!"

Taurus's words sent a chill down the spines of the women as they huddled in the laboratory. Their worst fears were realised, and they knew that somehow he was not bluffing.

They were still in a state of shock themselves, finding it hard to believe that there were armed men in the house, and holding their loved ones at gunpoint. They felt totally and utterly helpless, as one minute they had been standing in the kitchen thinking that the men had exaggerated the threat, and then, before they knew what had hit them, there had been an explosion. They were also feeling a sense of unreality, as they heard the chilling voice coming from the other side of the door, as they struggled to make a decision.

"Don't do it!"

Sagittarius managed to say something, as Taurus dug his foot into him, causing him to cringe with pain.

They could hear the emotion in his voice, and knew that he was in trouble.

"The professor's already been shot, and if you don't open the door, then I will shoot him again!"

Taurus held the barrel of his gun to Sagittarius's head, as Big Jim's mind began to clear.

"No!"

There was gasp from the laboratory as the seriousness of the situation hit them, just like the bullet that had hit Sagittarius.

They hated the feeling of helplessness, and in some way resented the fact that they had become helpless women. They were strong in their own right, and grasped firmly onto the taser guns that Big Jim had given them. Quite where he had got them from, and the risk he had taken in possessing them were thoughts that they put to the backs of their minds. They had them, which was the most important thing. Although, having a chance to use them was something else.

They would have to be very careful, as any wrong move would result in the death of the men, and that was the last thing that they wanted.

Astrid gathered her thoughts, trying to send out a calming energy, in the hope that the intruders would pick that up. She knew that it had worked in some similar cases, although the nano robots within their systems were blocking out normal emotions. All the intruders could think about was completing their mission, and if there were casualties, well then it was all part of the plan. They had been ready to kill, and to destroy the farm and any evidence too, and that was what they were going to do!

"Open the door!"

Taurus shouted his demand again, as his finger hovered over the trigger of his gun.

Looking at his son's blood stained clothes, and the ruthless stare of Taurus's eyes, Big Jim could see how determined he was. Resistance looked futile, and he was pinning his hopes on

Oracle, wondering when the friendly nano robots would gain control. He knew for definite that at least four of them had been injected, thanks to the lads, and he hoped that his son had managed to inject the other two, although he could not be certain.

"Do as he says."

Big Jim reluctantly caved in to Taurus's demands, hoping that it would be enough to save the life of his son. There was no point in aggravating him, as he looked as though underneath the mask he was a very unpleasant individual indeed, and one not to cross.

On the other side of the door, the women had organised themselves, and taken up positions on either side of the doorway. They had decided to open it, and the minute it was opened, they were all going to fire, hoping to incapacitate the intruders. It was a risky plan, but they felt as though they had to do something.

Big Jim could hear the sound of movement in the laboratory, as the furniture was being pulled away from the door. He realised that there was little choice, and hoped that everyone was going to get out of this alive. All of his years of research did not seem to matter any more, as the only important thing was the lives of those he cared about.

He looked at his son, who he loved, and could not bear to see him lying their with a gunshot wound. Sagittarius was brave and resourceful, and yet he regretted that his son had not run back to the laboratory and tried to tackle the men on his own.

"Move back, and don't try anything, or else they will die!"

Taurus's chilling words echoed through the hallway, as he signalled to Aquarius to open the door.

Astrid, Gemini and Caprica stood ready with their tasers in hand, and were about to fire, when the door opened, and they could see Sagittarius lying there with his blood stained shirt.

"Drop your weapons, and stand facing the wall."

There was a gasp as they saw Taurus, and the barrel of a gun pointing at Sagittarius's head.

They were shocked, and realising that there was nothing that they could do, reluctantly they did as they were told. Any thought of resistance had quickly faded, as there was no way of getting a clear shot at any of the intruders, and even if there had been, it looked as though the man holding the gun over Sagittarius would be able to get off the first shot. It looked hopeless, and once again they felt themselves reverting back to helplessness. So, they dropped their weapons, and walked calmly towards the far wall, facing it with their hands at their sides.

The men entered the room, and in a matter of seconds they all felt the harsh rub of plastic being pulled tight around their wrists. They could also see several guns pointed at their heads, and feared that they would be executed on the spot.

Taurus dragged Sagittarius into the laboratory, dropping him by the computer, whilst Virgo and Libra dragged Big Jim inside, dropping him by his son.

Oracle observed everything from his position on the work top, making out as if he was a real rabbit. He was busily coordinating everything, and twitched his whiskers as one of the men stared at him.

"I hate rabbits!"

Libra pointed his gun at Oracle, although fortunately did not fire. Oracle never flinched, although he was prepared to act if he sensed that the man would have actually fired. The workings of his processor were whirring away, and unbeknown to the intruders, he had already called the police.

Oracle had mimicked Big Jim's voice, and done it whilst everyone had been dashing about. He was hoping that help would arrive soon, and when it did, that the police were going to be able to do something.

It was now a hostage situation and, hopefully, he would be able to strike when the opportunity presented itself. He was also in contact with the *Lads*, who were monitoring things from outside. Everything was quiet out there, with the two men staying in position, one at the gate, and the other on the hillock.

Just as the intruders had entered the laboratory, he had also placed the security screen on the computer, as well as monitoring the friendly nano robots. He had readings from six different sources, all of which were operating at different levels. It looked as though the foreign nano robots had changed their frequencies slightly, obviously evolving. He had compensated, and the friendly nano robots were gaining the upper hand. It would still take a while for them to gain control, and it was important to give them as much time as he could.

If that was not enough to be getting along with, Oracle was also controlling the nano robots within Sagittarius's body. They had already managed to seal the wound and stop the bleeding, and were affecting repairs. It was incredible what they could do with the right set of commands, and it was very fortunate that he had so many within his body.

127

Now that he had stopped the bleeding, Oracle had also sent a command for some of them to attach themselves to the bullet, which was lodged in Sagittarius's shoulder. Miraculously, they had already started to eat their way into it, dissolving the metal into minute fragments, which would work their way naturally through his body. He was not out of the proverbial *woods* yet, but given enough time, he would make a full recovery.

Taurus's gruff voice barked out his latest order, drawing Libra's attention away from him

"You, get to that computer, and download as much information as you can."

Libra did as he was told, and sat at the computer, grabbing hold of the mouse. The screen was in lockout, as Oracle looked on innocently.

Libra tried to override the password, but after a few minutes he gave up, realising that his computer skills were no match for Big Jim's.

"I'm Locked out!"

Taurus looked less than pleased, stamping his foot on the floor in irritation.

"Give him the code!"

He pointed his gun at Sagittarius again, with his finger hovering back over the trigger. He knew that his father would not want to risk the life of his son, and whilst he had leverage over the scientist, he was determined to use it.

Looking at his son, Big Jim reluctantly decided that he had no choice, so gave them the code.

"Astrology."

Libra typed it in from the keyboard which sat beneath the monitor, and the screen came to life. He then reached into his pocket and pulled out several memory sticks, placing them into the USB slots, on the front of the desk-top tower.

"I'm in."

"Then download everything!"

Taurus barked out his orders, as Big Jim gave a big sigh. It looked as though despite their efforts, they had failed!

It was not much of a plan, and they had done their best. Coming up against six heavily armed professionals they had stood little chance. It now looked as though all of the information he had collated - a lifetime's work was going to fall into the wrong hands, and there was nothing that he could do about it!

The contents of the hard drive began to fill up the first of the memory sticks, and when that was full, Libra took it out, replacing it with another.

It was surprising how quickly the information was being passed, far too quickly for Big Jim's liking. His system was super fast, and he regretted making it run so smoothly. In a matter of hours, his research would have been transmitted, and in only a few short weeks time, everything that he had discovered would be used against all those who stood in the Organisation's way.

Everything appeared lost, until Taurus's radio sprang into life. It was Cancer.

"There is a police car heading down the lane in our direction!"

There was a sense of relief in the room as Big Jim looked at his wife, and the two young women. Perhaps help was on its way. He looked at Oracle, who twitched his whiskers at him, signalling that he had secretly made the call.

The men looked a bit worried, as Taurus put his hand up.

"Stay calm, I have things under control!"

He looked at his mobile phone, as it signalled that it had received a text.

CODE GREEN

He then called the men outside.

"Stay under cover, and await my instructions."

They did as they were ordered, disappearing into the night as the white *Armed Response Vehicle* sped along the lane, passing the parked black Land Rovers, its blue and yellow striped sides a blur as it neared the farm gates. Inside sat three officers, an Inspector, Sergeant and a Constable, all suitably dressed in protective clothing.

They had received the call earlier, and it was unusual for an Inspector to join the regular crew, in fact, everything about this particular call seemed a little strange...

For a start, it was as if the Inspector had been expecting something, as he had been hovering around all evening. Usually he was nowhere to be seen, unless there was an emergency. His presence made them feel uncomfortable, as his manner was abrupt, and seemed to be devoid of personality. There were those in the *service* who lived by the rule book, and others who were far more personable. Sadly he seemed to fit into the former, not the latter, and they had been made to feel on edge.

Then, there was the form which they had had to sign, stating that all front line officers were at risk of catching *tetanus*, and that they all needed a booster. Normally the police doctor would have dealt with that, but apparently he was too busy on this occasion.

They were both uncomfortable about having the injection, and it felt more like the army than the police force, as they were ordered to have it. Being injected by the Inspector did not seem right at all, and they had been grumbling to themselves outside whilst having a cigarette when the call came through. They were outranked, and neither of them had said anything, although the Sergeant had assured the Constable that he would have a quiet word in a friendly ear the following day.

That was however, for tomorrow, tonight was all about *Freedom Farm*, and even then, the details were a bit patchy. According to the Inspector, there was also another *Armed Response Unit* on its way from Bristol, but that would not get here for at least another half hour. From that snippet of information, they surmised that whatever it was had all of the hallmarks of being a serious incident.

A shadowy figure took cover behind the bushes as the car swerved in through the farm gate, rattling over the cattle grid as it sped down the driveway, coming to a halt by the old green Land Rover.

They seemed to be in the middle of nowhere, and as they all jumped out it appeared to be as quiet as the proverbial *grave*. They both had exactly the same thought, and their skin prickled as they felt eyes watching them from somewhere in the darkness.

Neither of them had felt quite the same after the injections, and they both shared a strange buzzing in their ears, and a very odd sort of an *unnatural* sense that something was very wrong. In their line of work they had to trust each other implicitly, as their lives depended on one another. Now, they both felt as though something had forced its way between them. For some reason they both felt a lack of trust, and exchanged apprehensive looks, as the Sergeant opened up the boot of the car, and removed their firearms from the secure storage locker bolted to the inside.

"Follow me!"

The Inspector gave out his order, as they each took a weapon and followed him up the side of the hillock, crouching down as they approached the ridge.

The farm looked very unusual, being mostly buried in the ground, and as they took a more detailed look at it with the aid of their night vision equipment, they noticed that one of the storm shutters had been blasted wide open. Some debris was littered across the courtyard, and it certainly looked as if there was an incident taking place.

They remained calm as they slipped down the hillock, running across the open ground until they found cover in the ornamental garden.

"Right, we're going in!"

The Inspector rose up and dashed towards the door as the other two covered him. He flung himself against the side, peering in through the hole the plastic explosive had made. It was a real mess, but as far as he could see, there was no one inside the kitchen.

"Move."

He signalled to the Sergeant who, gun in hand, squeezed his way through the shattered metal storm shutter, crunching over the broken glass, followed by the Constable.

Once both men had secured the room, the Inspector entered, surveying the damage. It looked to him as if plastic explosive had been used, as he had experience of using the stuff, having spent a few years in the army before joining the police force. He was not at all worried though, even if there were some heavily armed men hauled up inside.

They were being watched by Leo, who had taken cover on the roof. He had had them in his sights all of the time, but was obeying his orders not to fire.

The three police men entered the corridor, which again was deserted, and checked the lounge as they made their way along the corridor. The Sergeant noticed the bullet lodged in the shattered door frame, as well as traces of blood on the floor of one of the bedrooms, and a few more traces leading back out into the corridor.

He bent down to examine them a little more closely, and as he got up, he felt dizzy and stumbled to his feet. The Constable looked worried, as he was not feeling too good himself, both cursing the injection which they blamed for the way they felt.

The Inspector took no notice, ushering them on down the corridor, seemingly oblivious to the way they were feeling.

Big Jim could hear footsteps, as his hearing was still sharp, despite the blow to the head. His spirits were raised when he caught a glimpse of their uniforms, as he heard a voice shout.

"Police!"

Instead of a mad scramble, fire fight, or anything resembling what would have been normal for such a situation, there was calm. The men just lowered their weapons at Taurus's signal, as the policemen entered the room.

Big Jim was mystified, as the intruders took very little notice of the policemen. One minute it looked as though they were all going to be rescued, and the next, absolutely nothing!

It was the Inspector who spoke first, and when he did, it was certainly not what they had expected to hear.

"Have you got all of the information out yet?"

He spoke to Taurus, who gave Libra a nudge.

"Just another couple of minutes!"

Big Jim looked flabbergasted, and so did the others, not to mention the other two policemen. They really seemed to be struggling, and were very unsteady on their feet, having to prop themselves up against the wall. That did not last long, as within a few moments there was a grating sound, followed by crash, as they both collapsed on to the floor.

"Leave them, they will not bother us."

Taurus looked round, as the Inspector dismissed them with a flick of his wrist.

"They will come round later, and when they do, they will do exactly as I say."

His arrogant, uncaring words reverberated around the laboratory, as disbelief turned to shock. If Big Jim did not know any better, then he would have assumed that the Organisation had a man on the inside.

"Aren't you going to help us?"

His words were lost as the Inspector looked at him and sneered.

"It looks to me as if you have finally lost your mind, and attempted to kill your family. You will get at least ten years for the possession of a taser weapon, and life for the attempted murder of your son, wife and his girlfriends."

Big Jim looked horrified.

"What about those men?"

"What men, they will be gone in a few minutes."

"But the explosion, and my son?"

"It looks to me as if you did that yourself!"

"You will never get away with it!"

Big Jim was horrified.

"I already have!"

The Inspector then turned to face Sagittarius.

"It looks to me as if you are going to bleed to death, pity really as I understand that you had quite a promising career."

Sagittarius looked at him with contempt, too weak to do anything about it.

The Inspector then placed a call to London on his mobile telephone.

135

"Hello!"

A tired voice answered, as if the owner had been soundly asleep, and the call had awakened him.

"Operation concluded successfully."

There was a relieved sigh from the other end.

"Well done!"

"Thank you Sir!"

With that the Inspector rang off, looking rather smug.

Big Jim could not believe what he was hearing, and was shocked to see Libra pull the last of the memory sticks out of his computer, placing it in his pocket. He then signalled to Taurus who in turn signalled to the others that it was time for them to leave.

Fifteen

There was a deathly quiet in the laboratory, as the true seriousness of the situation began to sink in. Not only did Big Jim face a lengthy prison sentence, and the possibility of being placed in a mental institution, but all of his research, combined with information from the Department, as well as Sagittarius's research, would fall into the wrong hands too. Then there would be a breach in *National Security*, which would put the whole country at risk. The Organisation was international, so that meant that the technology would be used around the world, and other governments would also be at risk.

Things looked grim!

The Inspector however, looked smug, so smug in fact that he began to swagger.

"We will all be handsomely rewarded for this."

Greed seemed to be the main motivation, and any ethical values of upholding the good name of the Police Force had evaporated. The Inspector had *turned*, not just on the service and the country, but on the very people he was supposed to protect.

"So much for the rule of law!"

Big Jim muttered to himself.

"I am the law!"

The Inspector's arrogance knew no bounds.

"The law's an ass!"

The Inspector looked at him laughing.

"Well you're *ass* will not be seeing the light of day for a long while, if ever at all!"

The Inspector looked very pleased with himself, and the men laughed with him, thinking of the riches they were now going to enjoy. The Organisation rewarded success, equally as well as it punished failure.

Whilst the gloating continued, Oracle slipped unnoticed off the worktop, and hopped behind the two policemen, who were still lying in a heap on the floor. They had been discarded like an old newspaper, as the Inspector was making his own headlines.

Oracle gently pierced the skin of the Sergeant's wrist, injecting him with nano robots from his needle like teeth. He then hopped over to the Constable and did the same, as neither of them stirred. Then, scanning the room, he found himself somewhere to hide and disappeared in a corner behind some boxes.

"Good job, Taurus."

The Inspector congratulated the leader of the intruders, much to the disgust of the others in the room.

"Carry on, you have your orders."

Taurus stood to attention, and the men lined up behind him.

"I had better take your gun."

He handed it to the Inspector, who was going to use it as evidence, after it had been impregnated with Big Jim's fingerprints. In his mind, the Inspector already had everything worked out, even to the fact that he had disarmed a man who was about to kill his own family.

"Yes, Sir"

138

Taurus handed his gun over, before offering a salute. The Inspector saluted back, followed by the men.

"You had better get going, the other car will be here in a few minutes."

Taurus signalled to his men and they picked up their belongings heading for the door. There was nothing that Big Jim could do, and they all felt helpless. Sagittarius was awake and had heard everything, although he was making out as if he was still unconscious. The nano robots were busily repairing his wound, and the bullet had started to dissolve. He thought about trying to do something, but he realised that it was better if he waited until the men had gone.

The Inspector watched them go, holding onto the gun with his gloved hands. They had been careful, and there were no finger prints on it. He took a cloth out of his pocket and gave it a clean nevertheless, before removing the magazine. Then, when he was sure that he had removed all traces, he handed it to Big Jim, who refused to take it.

The Inspector held his own gun in his other hand, pointing it at Sagittarius.

"Either you hold it, or I will shoot him!"

Big Jim shook his head.

"How will you explain one of your bullets in my son?"

It was a good point, and the Inspector looked very annoyed.

"I'm sure that I can think of something!"

Big Jim frowned.

"Collateral damage!"

From the way he had been acting, he realised that he would put nothing past him, and whether or not he could get away with it, there was no use putting his son's life further at risk. So, reluctantly, Big Jim took the gun off him.

It was a defining moment, as he had just incriminated himself. The only saving grace was the fact that he had saved the life of his son.

The Inspector took it back off him, holding it with pride.

"Mission accomplished!"

Big Jim slumped back onto the floor, with an air of resignation. There would be a forensic examination, and hopefully the intruders had left their footprints and other traces that they had been here. That was the only hope that he could cling too, and the fact that everyone was still alive. Although, by the looks of the Inspector, and what had happened to the two officers, he had doubts whether the results of the forensic examination would not be tampered with. There was still hope, but that was cold comfort for the prospect of being locked up for months, if not years.

The women had remained quiet, being too shocked to say anything. It had not helped having a least one gun trained upon them all of the time. The men looked trigger happy, and they did not want to take any chances. Astrid had opened her mind, trying to send a calming energy. That had failed, as there was something blocking her thoughts. Usually she could reach into the minds of most people and sense what they were thinking and feeling. On this occasion, she seemed to be up against a brick wall. There was something inside the minds of all of the men, which seemed to have taken over their thoughts. They were being controlled, and it made her feel very uncomfortable.

The Inspector was not acting rationally either, and it was as though he was devoid of all emotions, apart from the negative ones. There was no point appealing to his better nature, as he did not appear to have one!

Gemini and Caprica felt totally helpless too, and inside their minds was a state of total and utter confusion. They could just not think clearly, and somehow had lost a large portion of their personalities. What was left was a muddle of thoughts and emotions, particularly as the man they had both grown so fond of was lying there wounded on the floor. They were clearly in shock, dazed and dumbfounded. The nano robots battling inside their bodies seemed to be pulling them in different directions, half of them still trying to obey the orders being transmitted to them, whilst the other half were trying to break free.

The months of conditioning was not going to be easy to get over, and all that they could think of was that they had to form an attachment to Sagittarius, and then bring him to the others. The others had now left, and just like when they were in Sagittarius's home, they were not sure of what to do next. Somehow, the previous few hours' events had taken them back, and their normal personalities were receding. There seemed to be a wall dividing them in half, and in some ways it felt like a prison. Each one wanted to break out, but they could not find a way of doing it. The turmoil inside their minds gathered pace, as they slumped down to the floor.

Astrid could see that they were in distress, but the moment she tried to move to help them, the Inspector waved his gun at them.

"Don't move or else I will shoot!"

So, she could do nothing but stand there helplessly.

There was a crunch of glass as the intruders jogged across the kitchen, squeezing through the storm door, and out into the courtyard. They were all buoyed by the success of their mission, with thoughts of a handsome reward when they made it back to London.

There was a rustle of bushes as Leo emerged form his cover, slipping down the grassed roof to join the others. No one spoke, as he slipped in behind them as they jogged up the other side of the hillock. He was pleased that they were finally on the move, having spent what seemed like ages crouching in the undergrowth.

Once they reached the summit, they had a clear view of the farm, as the sun began to prepare itself for the dawn, sending the first glints of light into the surrounding fields. One caught the solar panels, arranged in neat rows that gave the farm its power, whilst another caught the water of the reed beds, which processed all of the waste water. Ecology meant nothing to them, nor did the countryside. They were city dwellers, and could not wait to return to the hustle and bustle of busy streets. They were all glad to reach the driveway, and enjoyed stretching their legs as they ran up towards the gate.

Cancer rose himself up from the bushes to greet them, and joined the end of the single line of men as they crossed the cattle grid with clangs of metal.

The lane was deserted as they started the short jog towards the black Land Rovers. They would all be glad to climb inside, and get away from here before the other police car arrived. The Inspector had everything under control, and they had done their job. The Organisation would be pleased, which made up for the failure of operations earlier.

Sagittarius had given them the slip, but now, in their eyes he had got his just rewards. They doubted whether he would ever bother them again, and they had also got his father's research, which more than made up for their earlier failure.

Libra had the memory sticks zipped in his jacket pocket, so the mission had been a complete success.

A few birds began to stir as the sound of their boots on the tarmac disturbed them. Dawn was fast approaching, and the chorus was about to get into full swing.

There was a glint of sunlight reflecting off the Land Rovers' windscreens, as they came into view, and in only a few short minutes they were at the lay-by.

Once they arrived, their equipment was quickly stashed in the back, and almost before the last door was closed, the engines were started and they had began to pull out of the lay-by. In the distance a set of lights could be seen, coming up quickly behind them, and it looked as though they had set off just in the nick of time. With lights off, they drove past the farm gates, and around the first corner, disappearing out of sight as the police car came screeching to a halt.

Sixteen

There was an uneasy quiet in the police car, as both occupants surveyed the land. The Sergeant and Constable looked at one another, and then at the old green Land Rover, followed by the other police car from a fellow *Armed Response Unit*. All looked quiet, too quiet for their liking!

"What do you make of this, Sarge?"

The Sergeant shrugged his shoulders. It looked to him as if they were sitting in the middle of a field.

"We'd better get an update."

He pressed the button on the radio strapped to his lapel.

"Armed Response Unit in position, requesting further information."

There was a buzz from his radio as a voice replied.

"This is Inspector Trust, I have the situation under control."

"Trust!"

Big Jim raised his eyebrows.

"That takes the biscuit!"

If ever there was someone with a less appropriate name, then it had to be the Inspector!

"I have apprehended the suspect - a Scientist who has lost his mind and tried to kill his entire family."

Big Jim frowned, as they all looked at him in disbelief, and more than a little disgust.

"Proceed into the building and meet me in the laboratory."

"Yes, Sir!"

The Sergeant turned to face his colleague.

"Looks like a domestic has got out of control."

They both shrugged, getting slowly out of their car, moving to the rear of the vehicle and, once the boot was opened, they retrieved their weapons from the sealed locker inside.

"Follow me."

The Sergeant led the way as they followed the little gravel path that stretched out from the driveway, and up and over the hillock that housed the complex.

"Looks more like a *break in* to me than a *domestic*."

The Constable commented as they saw the damage to the storm shutter, and all of the debris lying about.

"Someone must have been using explosives."

The Sergeant had over twenty years experience, and had been with *Tactical Firearms* for over seven. It was an interesting job, quite dangerous at times, but better than pounding the beat, or riding around in a patrol car all day.

The Constable was quite new to this, only having a few months experience. To him it was still exciting, as he was relatively young, having only been in the service for five years.

They neared the patio, with its shattered sculptures and layer of debris. They could clearly see the hole in the steel shutter, and drawing their weapons, they advanced.

The kitchen was a real mess, with a layer of glass, broken crockery, and assorted pieces of cooking equipment covering the floor. There was a broken lap top computer on the table, which looked as though someone had picked it up and tried to get it working. That was puzzling, as they tried to see in the dark, with the only light that of the hallway, and a few strands from the approaching dawn venturing in through the shutter.

The Sergeant pointed at the Constable to cover him, as he advanced into the hallway. All was quiet as they proceeded to check each room in turn until they noticed the blood on the door frame of one of the bedrooms, and the bullet lodged in the shattered wood above.

That caused a few raised eyebrows, and making a mental note, they moved on cautiously until they approached the laboratory.

The Inspector was waiting for them, and they had a bit of a shock when they poked their heads around the door.

On the floor lay two of their colleagues, and the Inspector was holding his gun over a large hippie-looking man with a pot belly and bushy grey beard. Near them lay another man who appeared to have been shot, and on the far side there were three women. One, a slim attractive middle aged woman was standing over two very attractive younger women, who seemed to be in a state of distress.

The Inspector pointed his head in Big Jim's direction.

"This ageing scientist has lost his mind and tried to kill his family. When we arrived, we found that they had shut themselves in here. He must have got hold of some explosives as he blasted his way inside. I have recovered several taser weapons, and this rifle, which he used to shoot his son."

He nodded toward Sagittarius, who clearly had a gun-shot wound to his shoulder.

"I disarmed him, but he managed to taser those two before I could get the situation under control."

"It's all a pack of lies!"

Big Jim protested.

"As you can see, there is always a fine line with these scientist types between genius and insanity. Something must have finally pushed him over the edge. By the look of him, he appears to have been a bit on the eccentric side at the best of times."

Big Jim's appearance did give them food for thought.

"All he would say is that there is a conspiracy - a plot to take over the world!"

The Inspector laughed, mockingly.

"So, what you are saying Inspector, is that he has lost his mind."

The Inspector nodded.

"I'm sane, it's the Inspector who's crazy!"

"Yes, that's right!"

Astrid joined in.

"We were attacked by a group of armed men, all dressed in black combat gear. The Inspector is in cahoots with them."

"A classic case of a family trying to cover up the truth."

The Inspector dismissed her comments.

"She is telling the truth."

Gemini and Caprica joined in.

Sagittarius opened his eyes. He had been resting as the nano robots made repairs to his body. They had successfully sealed the wound which was healing nicely, and had already dissolved a portion of the bullet.

"Professor Sagittarius, head of Experimental department, MI6"

He reached into his jacket pocket, pulling out his identity card.

"The Inspector is a fraud!"

The two policemen looked at each other. There was definitely something amiss. Why would they all fabricate the same story, and why was there someone here claiming to be from MI6?

"It all seems a bit fishy to me Sarge!"

The Constable was not the only one having doubts, as the Sergeant looked at the Inspector.

"Are you sure, Sir?"

"I am in charge, are you doubting my word?"

The Sergeant shook his head.

"No, Sir!"

"Well then, attend to those two, whilst I keep you covered.

They moved over to their two colleagues, who were beginning to come round. The Inspector was confident that the injection had worked, and that they would back him up. However, he did not realise that they had also received counter nano robots thanks to Oracle.

"Oh my head!"

The Sergeant was the first to awaken, quickly followed by the Constable.

"What happened?"

He was still a little dazed, and his mind was all fuzzy.

"I was hoping that you could tell me!"

The other Sergeant did not know what to think. It certainly did not look like a normal domestic, in fact it was the strangest call that he had ever had!

"I don't remember much, and what I do remember does not make much sense to me."

"What about you, lad?"

The Constable, who was much younger, also struggled to remember.

"Everything's been a bit of a blur since the injection."

"What injection?"

The Constable told him about the tetanus jabs.

"It's an order that's come from the top."

The Inspector reached into his jacket pocket, pulling out some paperwork, and hidden within it was a syringe.

"look, its all here."

He moved forward towards the Sergeant, and when he was in range, he pulled the protective cover off the needle and jabbed it into the Sergeant's arm.

"What are you doing?"

The Sergeant pulled back as he felt the jab pierce his flack jacket.

"Taking over!"

149

He dropped the syringe and paperwork, quickly grabbing the Sergeant's gun, pointing it at him.

It all happened too quickly for the Constable to react, and when he did, he could see that the Inspector was holding a gun to the Sergeant's head.

"Drop your weapon, and that's an order!"

The Constable hesitated, but when his Sergeant gave him the nod, he did what he was told.

"Now pick up that syringe and inject yourself with it, or I will shoot him!"

The Constable stood where he was until the Inspector waved his gun towards him. That gave Sagittarius just enough time to act. From his position on the ground, he used his feet to shove the Inspector off balance, and as he staggered, the gun went off.

The sound of the shot reverberated around the laboratory, as Oracle leapt out from behind the boxes, firing his taser at the Inspector, who dropped to the ground, letting go of his gun as he fell.

Sagittarius caught it before it hit the ground, and as the Inspector hit the floor, he was able to point it at his head.

The Constable leapt forward and grabbed him, reaching into his pocket and pulling out his handcuffs. There was a click as he fastened them round the Inspector's wrists. He then breathed out a huge sigh of relief. It all seemed to have happened so quickly, and he was very thankful for Sagittarius's actions.

Seventeen

Dawn finally broke as the birds chirped merrily in the trees and hedgerows, totally unaware of the drama being played out beneath the hillock. To the untrained eye it looked like the perfect example of tranquillity and calm. The farm lay in rolling countryside, an eco construction that did nothing to pollute the environment. In actual fact, apart from the solar panels, there was very little sign of habitation at all. Even the driveway, which led up from the farm gate was made of gravel with a few blades of grass sticking up out of the centre, between the ruts made by the Land Rover's tyres. It sat outside a set of garage doors, with the garage itself submerged into the hillock, like all of the other buildings.

That was a very normal sight, and even it being dark green sat comfortably within the field. What was unusual was the fact that there were two police cars parked next to it, belonging to the *Tactical Fire Arms* squads. They had long since left their vehicles, and climbed the gravel pathway up the side of the hillock and down into the courtyard.

Normally the stone flagged surface was neat and tidy, with its sculptures and assorted plants looking like something out of a glossy gardening magazine. That was not the sight that greeted the regular patrol car's occupants, and the ambulance crew that had accompanied them. Peace had been shattered by the sound of sirens, and the normally tranquil scene of a few moments ago quickly turned to bedlam.

With a grinding of gravel, both vehicles sped up the driveway, skidding to a halt by the other vehicles. The stomp of boots and the rattle of equipment hurrying up the slope sent the birds screeching and diving for cover.

The explosion had ripped apart years of careful collecting and planting, leaving a decapitated statue of a goddess and other pieces of fragmented art lying about, as if caught up in some unnatural maelstrom.

That was indeed the case, as the new day had brought hope, and the old saying that *it is always darkest before the dawn*, was never more apt for the Sagittarius family.

Inside their rather unusual home there had occurred the most unusual experience of their lives, which was proving difficult to come to terms with, and even more difficult to explain.

All of the responsibility fell on the shoulders of one police Constable, who, when he started the night shift, never dreamed for one moment that he would have been involved in such an incident.

Not only had he discovered that an Inspector had turned traitor, but three of his colleagues had been injured by an injection containing something that was far beyond his level of understanding. Then there was an ageing hippie who turned out to be one of the worlds leading Scientists, his wife who was an *Alternative Therapist*, a Professor from MI6 and his two girl friends!

It was going to be quite a report that he would be making later!

Sagittarius stood up, his head finally clear, and his wound almost totally healed. That was something else that was going to be hard to explain, plus the fact that a rabbit had sprung up from behind some boxes and shot a taser at the Inspector from one of his front paws.

The Constable wished that he had been off duty and that someone else had received last night's call.

It was with a great deal of relief that he saw the regular police running towards him followed by the ambulance crew. He just stepped aside as they entered the laboratory.

"What's been going on here then?"

The Sergeant asked, looking around at the very strange scene that greeted him. The Constable took a deep breath, not quite knowing where to start. The Sergeant had his pocket book out, and the flap dangled as he reached for his pen.

"Well…"

Before he could continue, Sagittarius showed him his card, stating that the whole investigation fell under the jurisdiction of *National Security*. Someone was on their way from the Department, to oversee the whole thing, as the Sergeant's pen remained poised over his pocket book.

The ambulance crew worked their way around the room, untying everyone and checking them over. Big Jim felt the greatest relief, as it was not that long ago that he faced the very real prospect of being locked in a mental institution for the rest of his life. That prospect was something that had filled him with dread!

Astrid was hugging him, and he doubted whether she would ever remove her vice like grip again. Sagittarius was also being hugged, as two pairs of arms pressed two pairs of large breasts against him, making him feel more than a little uncomfortable. Being saved from this situation was one thing, but being saved from the clutches of two infatuated women was going to be something entirely different!

The policemen were now up and about, apart from the Sergeant who had been injected. His head throbbed, although the

153

counter injection was helping. A large black rabbit was also hopping about, and the sound from the corridor signalled the arrival of another ten.

Big Jim could still hear the Inspector's voice claiming that he had finally lost his mind and his family had locked themselves away from him in fear of their lives, that he had used plastic explosive to break into his own home, and that he was going to find a way of proving where he had acquired it and the tasers. He had in fact purchased them, and held them illegally, which was still a worry. How was he going to explain that?

He felt sure that the Inspector would have found a way of making him sign a false confession too, and taken all of the glory for his arrest. Maybe people did think that he was a little crazy, and that somehow he would have been able to make his family testify against him. After all, who actually knew how persuasive one of those injections could be?

He shuddered at the thought!

The Inspector had nearly got away with it!

Far in the distance, the morning rush hour was gaining pace along the M4 as two black Land Rovers entered the outskirts of London. Their occupants were buoyed by their success and looking forward to a substantial reward. All they really cared about was money, and the more they had, the happier they became.

It was not always that way, but after being recruited by the Organisation, all of their lives had changed. That was the thing about the nano robots, they took over a person's personality, changing it as their programming dictated. Hidden away, the

154

mastermind of the entire operation sat in a secret location. The figure was very mysterious, and even the Organisation did not know his real identity.

Posing as a computer hacker, all traces of him led to a dead end, as all tracks had been well and truly covered, and the identity was protected by a very elaborate smoke screen. The only method of contact was via a mobile telephone, whose signal was bounced off various devices that made tracing the call virtually impossible, and via email. It was the same with the email address too, which was linked to a fictitious account. Payment was made to an offshore account in the name of a Mr Smith, which again was yet another alias.

Arachnid had originally made contact after receiving information that there was a master hacker somewhere, who was the best in the business. He had placed an advert on a hacking website simply stating that for *certain services* payment would be *handsome. Handsome*, was a word which repeatedly cropped up, and one which the Organisation liked to use. The definition meant dignified, dexterous and well rewarded, terms which they liked to be associated with. Devious, ruthless, and control were also traits of the secret organisation that spanned several continents. Quite who and where the hacker was, was not important, just the fact that the job was done to the Organisation's satisfaction. Failure was not a word which they liked to use, or tolerate!

The only reference that they had was the codename *Dark Star,* which seemed appropriate considering that they were all using astrological pseudonyms. This was, however, just one tentacle of a beast which lay hidden in the shadows, ready to strike out or extend its reach whenever it wished!

Dark Star monitored the signals from the men, each displayed on a large computer screen. Expectations were high that the information they carried would soon be delivered. There was however, displeasure with the Police Inspector, and action had to be taken.

The nano robot sensors not only transmitted brain wave activity, but also when they were moved into position they could also interact with the brain's visual cortex. This was not an easy process, but Dark Star's sensors detected foreign nano robots within his body. It appeared that he had been compromised, and there was a chance that he might reveal some vital information.

There was the inevitable time delay, and things were made even more difficult than usual by the interference of the other nano robots, as they began to tackle the existing ones within his body. By his own estimates, Dark Star calculated that he would have only minutes of control left. His computer screen displayed a momentary image transmitted by the Inspector's eyes of his wrists bound in handcuffs. That was enough for him, confirmation that he had failed in his mission.

It was now only a matter of time before he regained some control over his mind, and when he did, there was only one logical conclusion - betrayal!

That was something which the Organisation would not tolerate, as failure was not an option. Without the slightest hesitation, Dark Star submitted the fail safe code, which bounced of a satellite, returning to earth a few moments later.

The Inspector was now sitting in the back of a police car, handcuffed and accompanied by another policeman. The atmosphere was tense as the Inspector sat silently, dazed and more than a little confused. He was getting flashbacks of things which he had done, but did not make any sense to him, fleeting memories of his earlier career, and others which he found very difficult to believe. He was not sure whether he had done what he was remembering, and looking down at his wrists, he felt disbelief. Why was he sitting handcuffed in the back of the police car?

His mind was awash with secret transmissions, coded messages, instructions of a secret meeting with a strange doctor, and of an injection which seemed to have changed his life forever.

What had happened to him?

There were also pains in his head which seemed to be getting worse, as though there was something digging into his brain. The pain was getting more intense by the second, and he felt like he was going to explode. Then, before he knew what had happened, he slumped unconscious on the seat.

Dark Star showed no emotions and felt none either, conscience was not part of the plan, nor the Organisation's. The Inspector had been dealt with, which safeguarded security, and attention was now turned towards the rest of the men.

Had they also been compromised?

That was a big question, and to cover such an eventuality, the order was given to inject themselves with another dose of nano robots just in case. The men suddenly had the thought that they needed to inject themselves, and so as soon the thought was placed in their minds, syringes were removed from the glove compartment and handed out. Each man injected himself by rolling up a sleeve, feeling little reaction as they took hold. The tide of war within their systems had turned, just as it appeared that they might be able to regain control of their minds.

There was now no chance of that, although unbeknown to Dark Star, some information had already leaked out.

Back in the laboratory, whilst everyone hugged and relief spread around the room, Oracle was still busy and had managed to access the numbers stored in Taurus's mobile telephone, that Sagittarius had taken out of his pocket in the hallway of their home. There was one number which he had great interest in, and he was already busily trying to trace where it originated from. It was not going to be easy to trace the caller, but Oracle was very resourceful and concentrated all of his efforts on this one task.

Back in the Land Rovers, Taurus had absolutely no idea what was going on in the outskirts of Glastonbury; as far as he was concerned the operation had been a complete success. He had not given it a second thought, when his mobile telephone had gone missing, as they had all acquired new ones before the operation.

There was only one task left, and that was to deliver the memory sticks containing all of the information Dark Star required. Having already acquired a very good knowledge of the subject, these would help to advance knowledge even further. Having a foothold in British Intelligence was the next step, as there was already a mole in the American secret services. Dark Star was driven by the desire for revenge, and vengeance was the emotion that drove more than any other. The ultimate goal was power, and as *Lord Acton* had once remarked *Power tends to corrupt, and absolute power corrupts absolutely; great men were almost always bad men.* In this particular case, that made for the Organisation's perfect recruit.

It could have been simpler to have had the hard drive removed from Big Jim's computer, but cracking the security code presented no real problems. Downloading information had taken time, but there was no real hurry. Memory sticks were versatile and having a virus embedded within one of them meant continual access to whatever information lay within Big Jim's computer. It was simple to introduce, and everything had been thought out meticulously. The Organisation liked that sort of thing, and everything had proceeded more or less according to plan.

Losing the Inspector was unfortunate, but another recruit could be gained whenever the need arose. Not terminating Sagittarius was a disappointment, although he could still be removed at a later date.

It was now just a case of waiting for the men to arrive in London, where one of them would mail the memory sticks to a post office address in a padded envelope. It would be far less traceable if done in the city, and as he waited, the Land Rovers entered the early rush hour traffic.

Thoughts were still concentrated on reward as they came to a halt behind a line of traffic, and with a certain satisfaction, they saw that there was a red post box sitting on the pavement next to the first vehicle. It was simple to jump out and slip the padded envelope in through the slot, with its prepaid postage. Being virtually untraceable, there was no risk to security.

That was the last part of the operation, and the men would all split up as soon as they reached an underground station, with the drivers returning the vehicles to lock up garages, ready for the false plates to be removed and a new coat of paint added. Within a few short hours the two black Land Rovers would have disappeared altogether.

There was indeed an underground station nearby, and the combat uniforms were quickly removed as they were only held together via Velcro strips. Underneath the men wore civilian clothes, and their discarded uniforms were bagged ready for disposal. Soon there would be absolutely nothing to connect them with tonight's operation, and as they neared the underground station, four of them jumped out, leaving the drivers to proceed alone.

Dark Star monitored their signals, as they deleted their call history from their mobile phones before depositing them in rubbish bins along the high street. New ones had been sent in the post as usual, waiting for them when they returned to their homes.

Just over a hundred miles away, the ambulance crew stood mystified, as they examined Sagittarius's shoulder. It was not the first time that they had treated a gun shot wound, and they were amazed at how quickly this particular one was healing. Normally such an injury would require them to stop the bleeding, and would then need surgery. However, somehow it looked as though it was healing itself, and unnaturally quickly too!

He would have to be taken to hospital nevertheless, and when they eventually prized Gemini and Caprica away from him, he calmly accompanied them as they made the walk along the corridor toward the kitchen. There was no way that the two young women were going to leave him, and they hurried along behind, much to the amusement of the ambulance crew.

This was a very strange call, and now that MI6 was apparently involved, they knew better than to ask too many questions.

That was just as well, as looking at each other, they decided that it was probably for the best!

Bright sunshine greeted them as they emerged from the kitchen, and as they made their way across the shattered courtyard towards the path, they were met by a man in a sombre dark suit. Nods were exchanged but nothing was said as he walked calmly towards the hole in the storm shutter.

At the other end of the path an unmarked black car with dark tinted windows was parked next to the ambulance, and there were no prizes for guessing that it was now officially a matter of National Security.

The ambulance crew opened the back doors of their vehicle and Sagittarius helped Gemini and Caprica up the steps, before calmly joining them, as one of the men closed the door behind him. The ambulance crew then exchanged bemused glances, before walking to the front.

The sunshine was already spreading its warmth, as the engine started and they reversed back before pulling forward. This had been quite a night shift, and they would both be glad when it was finally over!

The ambulance glided along the driveway and rattled over the cattle grid as it entered the lane, soon passing the lay-by where the black Land Rovers had been parked only an hour before.

They were heading for the main hospital and under strict orders not to speak about what they had seen. That was just as well, as no one would have believed them if they had. What with secret agents, mad professors, aging hippies and nearly a dozen very strangely behaving black rabbits, they began to doubt it themselves!

161

Bristol Royal Infirmary was a hive of activity as the ambulance pulled into one of the bays, with relief spreading over the crew's faces. Soon they would be free of their guests, and hopefully after a well earned sleep they could put everything behind them.

The hospital was busy as usual, and after making their way through Accident and Emergency, Sagittarius and the two young women found themselves in a private room. Outside staff and patients milled around unaware that inside, a member of MI6 lay on a bed with a confused doctor looking at his charts, and examining an X Ray. He scratched his head not believing what he was seeing. Instead of his patient having to go to surgery to have a bullet removed, it had almost completely dissolved naturally. The wound had similarly healed beyond all expectation, and his mind drifted back to his childhood favourite program *Captain Scarlet and the Mysterons*. His patient seemed to have a most remarkable immune system, and in all of his years in medicine he had never seen anything quite like it.

There was a knock at the door, which opened slowly, and there stood an ageing hippy with a big bushy beard, and a slim attractive women who he took to be his wife.

"May we come in?"

The doctor waved them through, still looking at the charts in disbelief.

"Will he live?"

Big Jim already knew the answer.

"Mr and Mrs Sagittarius I presume?"

The doctor could see the family resemblance and began to understand why his patient seemed to have two girlfriends, and identical twins at that - they got all sorts in this hospital!

His patient did not look like a hippie, as he had been wearing a smart suit, but he was unusual nevertheless.

"Judging by his rate of recovery, I would not be surprised if he lived forever!"

Everyone smiled, none more so than Gemini and Caprica. Sagittarius still felt very uneasy about the whole situation as they looked at him with adoring eyes. What was he going to do about them?

The doctor replaced the charts, shaking his head, and wishing that he could duplicate his patient's immune system. He had to treat a lot of very sick people, and some of their lives he had not been able to save. If only he could duplicate whatever it was within Sagittarius's body, then he would be able cure virtually everyone he saw.

Still deep in contemplation, he left the room after telling them that his patient would soon be discharged, much to the relief of everyone concerned.

The family now gathered around Sagittarius's bedside, happy in the knowledge that their ordeal was finally over.

"I'm glad that you're OK, son."

Sagittarius smiled.

"It's just a shame that they got away with all of our research."

Big Jim gave him *one of those* looks.

"Whoever accesses it will be in for a big surprise!"

They all looked at him.

"I still have one or two tricks up my sleeve!"

Sagittarius did not doubt that for a second!

"Do you think that we have seen the last of those men?"

Astrid was still concerned, as she bent down and kissed her son on the cheek.

"I should think so!"

He did not want to worry his mother, although secretly he knew that their paths would inevitably cross again.

"What makes people do such a thing?"

He shrugged his shoulders.

"Why can't everyone just live in peace and harmony?"

Sagittarius could see the genuine hope in his mother's eyes.

Big Jim put his arm around his wife.

"Unfortunately, there's no Utopia, never has been and never will be, the human condition prevents it. There is always someone who wants more than others, wishes to control them, whether by fair means or foul. Even those who start off with the highest ideals fall by the wayside as they get corrupted or find themselves coerced into doing things which they do not wish to do - as a species we just can't help ourselves!"

Astrid looked at him as he held up his newspaper in his other hand. Fortunately there was no report on the happenings at Freedom Farm, although there was the usual scare story emblazoned with big letters on the front.

164

"Fear is the greatest weapon known to man, and there is nothing more powerful than a National fear. First it was the *Cold War*, then *Terrorists*, followed by *Asteroids*, and finally it will be *Aliens*, and the saddest thing of all is that it is all a lie!"

He tightened his grip on Astrid.

"Just call me an old cynic."

He kissed her on the top of her head.

"All we can do is to do our best to change the Status Quo!"

Deep down, they knew that he was right.

Change, however, was on its way...

Back in the Gentleman's Club, a waiter quietly walked towards the discreet booth occupied by two of the clubs members. In his hand he held a silver tray containing a small card. When they saw him approaching, their conversation died, and the first man looked up at him, wondering what he wanted.

The waiter lowered the tray.

"Excuse me Sir, I have a police Inspector asking to see you..."

Thank you for reading my book

If you enjoyed this read, please leave a review on Amazon. It only takes a few minutes and it really does make a difference.

Just click here to go to my author's page.

At the side of the title click on see more, and scroll down until you see customer reviews

Click on write a customer review and click on the stars

Thank you so much!

www.ingramcontent.com/pod-product-compliance
Lightning Source LLC
Chambersburg PA
CBHW070925130626
46555CB00001B/292